The Adventures of
# PUNKIN AND BOO
—— Third Edition ——

# THE MYSTERY OF GHOST DANCER RANCH

## BOOK ONE

# ENDORSEMENTS

A delightful tale of mystery, adventure and suspense, *The Mystery of Ghost Dancer Ranch* is an engaging story you don't want to miss.
—**Paul Regnier**, author of *Paranormia* and *Space Drifters*.

*The Mystery of Ghost Dancer Ranch* took me back to my childhood love of Nancy Drew, but it also included a unique blend of both historical and supernatural elements to make it even more intriguing.
—**Angela Ruth Strong**, award-winning author of *The Water Fight Professional*

Patrick E. Craig is an excellent writer. He weaves tales with heart, imagination, and a healthy dose of mystery. I'm always excited to see what he'll do next.
—**Lindsay A. Franklin**, author of *The Story Peddler*, Realm Award Book of the Year 2019

The Adventures of
**PUNKIN AND BOO**
—— Third Edition ——

# THE MYSTERY OF GHOST DANCER RANCH

## BOOK ONE

## PATRICK E. CRAIG

PUBLISHING THE POSITIVE

ELK LAKE PUBLISHING INC
Plymouth, Massachusetts

Cover and Interior Design: Mickey Leonard, Derinda Babcock
Editor(s): Jeanne Marie Leach, Deb Haggerty
Author Represented By: Steve Laube Agency

PUBLISHED BY: Elk Lake Publishing, Inc., 35 Dogwood Drive, Plymouth, MA 02360, 2019

Library Cataloging Data
Names: Craig, Patrick E. (Patrick E. Craig)
*The Adventures of Punkin and Boo: Book One—The Mystery of Ghost Dancer Ranch* | Patrick E. Craig
124 p. 23cm × 15cm (9in × 6 in.)
Description: Cousins Punkin and Boo discover a mystery at their grandparents' ranch.
Identifiers: ISBN-13: (trade) | 978-1-951080-39-6 (POD)
| 978-1-951080-40-2 (e-book)
Key Words: Middlle-grade, Native Americans, traditions, Mafia, Casinos, Problem-solving,
LCCN: 2019949171 Fiction

# DEDICATION

To my granddaughters, Hannah and Jacie—may they have God adventures all their lives

# CONTENTS

# PREFACE

*The Mystery of Ghost Dancer Ranch* came about through an interesting set of circumstances. One night, I had a dream in which a favorite aunt who had always encouraged my writing appeared. With a well-remembered, stern look in her eye, she pointed her finger at me and said, "You write!"

The next morning, as I read the local paper, I noticed an ad in the classifieds: "For Sale, The Ghost Dancer Ranch." The whole story literally came to me in a moment, and I set about to write the book the next day. The year was 2007, *The Mystery of Ghost Dancer Ranch* was my first book, and I've been on the writing journey ever since.

# ACKNOWLEDGMENTS

To my wife, Judy, for her tireless efforts in proofing and editing
*The Mystery of Ghost Dancer Ranch*

To Sue Loeffler, for being the first to encourage me in the writing
of this book and for keeping me in the active voice.

To Dan Kline, for his friendship and support and guidance in the
writing process.

# CHAPTER ONE
## THE OLD RANCH

Fourteen-year-old Hannah Roberts leaned on the sill and looked through the small panes of the second-story window in the old farmhouse. She frowned. "Oh pancakes! Another gray day."

The fog had blown in again loaded with moisture from the cold Pacific. The cypress trees along the fence line dripped and looked mournful. The mist condensed on the window and ran down over the outer sill in errant rivulets to attack the peeling paint on the outside of the house. Grandpa had told her the ranch was well over one hundred years old, and it definitely showed today.

Hannah frowned and leaned her face on her hands as she watched the billowing fog stream by. "I've been in Petaluma almost a week, and we haven't had one sunny day," she said to her reflection. "Of all the places in the world, how did I end up in California for the summer? I miss my friends."

"Boo, breakfast is ready, honey," her grandma called up the stairs.

The thought of Grandma's cooking cheered her up, and she appreciated Grandma calling her Boo like her folks did. Grandma's quick acceptance of her took the edge off her homesickness for Michigan. Hannah sighed, turned from the window, and got dressed. Unfortunately, she could do nothing about her situation. Her dad had an offer for a good job in Texas, so she was staying with her grandparents while her parents looked for a new home.

# The Mystery of Ghost Dancer Ranch

Hannah hated the thought of moving from Michigan. All her friends were there, and she had been getting ready for the riding competition at the stable where she took lessons when her Mom gave her the news. She missed her youth group at the church. *This trip ruins my whole summer! You'd think I could at least have a sunny day to make up for it.*

The only good thing she could think of about being here was her cousin, Jacie Masters, coming for a two-week visit.

*I hope she's not stuck-up. I could really use a friend right now.*

Pulling on her sweatshirt, she started down to the kitchen. As she went along the hallway lined with faded pictures and family portraits, Boo realized she liked the old house. The day her folks dropped her off, Grandpa had taken her for a tour of the ranch. She had a "thing" for old buildings and mysterious settings, and the old ranch house had those.

The Ghost Dancer Ranch house sat on a level spot halfway up a knoll in the middle of sixteen hundred acres of land between Petaluma and the coastal hills. Grandma told Boo about an earlier Spanish-era structure on the same spot that burned down, leaving only a stone fireplace and a chimney. After Great-Great-Grandfather Jamison bought the property, he built the house using the fireplace as part of the structure. He updated the old fireplace with modern brickwork and made it the centerpiece of the huge dining room. The winding road leading up to the knoll and ending in a circular driveway in front of the house reminded Boo of an old southern mansion.

Tall cypress trees on the back slope of the knoll acted as a break against the wind blowing in every afternoon through the gap in the western hills. The house had a somewhat ramshackle appearance because of all the rooms added over the years yet was still beautiful in an old-fashioned way. A wide porch swept around the front of the house, and broad stairs led up to the doublewide front door. Pillars held the old porch roof up below her bedroom window. Boo had already planned on sneaking out and climbing down the post to go exploring at night.

The second story was a maze of rooms, and the top of the house had a huge attic with a widow's walk looking out toward the ocean. To the west, the fields rose into the foothills of the coastal range lined with forests of eucalyptus and pines and tall, bald outcrops of rocks. Grandpa said there were good riding trails, and Boo was eager to saddle up the grey mare he kept in the pasture. Northward, the land broke up into canyons winding crookedly up to the top of the ridge. Out of these, small streams fed into the pond beyond the big pasture.

On her first day at the ranch, her grandpa took her out to the pond and showed her the diving board and the shed full of fishing gear.

He looked up at the gray clouds and shrugged his shoulders. "We'll have swimming and fishing if the sun ever comes out."

Altogether, the ranch was an interesting place. When they had driven through the gate, Boo noticed the little sign, "Welcome to Ghost Dancer Ranch," and she made a mental note to ask Grandma about the name, She skipped the last two steps of the back stairwell coming down from the second story and landed in the kitchen.

Grandma bustled about, frying up bacon and eggs. She smiled. "Who were you talkin' to up there?"

"Just myself again, Grandma." Hannah sat down and grinned sheepishly.

"Don't worry, sweetie." Her grandmother laughed and patted her on the head. "Jacie will be here soon so you'll have someone else to talk to. Now grab your milk. Eggs will be ready in a minute."

Boo poured a big glass of fresh milk and took a long, satisfying drink. "Grandma, why do they call this place Ghost Dancer Ranch?"

"Well, Boo," her grandma said as she looked over from the stove. "One of the last of the great Indian Ghost Dancers came here in

1891 and hid out on the ranch. Ever since then the locals always called the place Ghost Dancer Ranch."

"What's a Ghost Dancer, Grandma?" Hannah's curious bone was being tickled.

"Finish your breakfast and I'll tell you the story." Grandma slid the eggs on to Hannah's plate.

After breakfast, Boo followed Grandma into the small room off the kitchen which served as Grandma's sewing room and office. She watched as Grandma rummaged around in the closet until she found an old box she brought out and opened. Inside were newspaper clippings which she spread out on her desk.

Boo could read some of them. *Ghost Dancer Rebellion Comes to California* blazoned one headline.

Grandma pointed to another. *Ghost Dancer Red Bull Captured in Ukiah.* "You may not know this, but our family on my dad's side is part Sioux Indian. My dad was one-half Sioux, so you are one-sixteenth. Our ancestors belonged to the Horse Tribes of the Great Plains who fought the white soldiers in defense of their tribal homelands."

"You mean like Crazy Horse and Sitting Bull and all the famous Indians we see on the history channel?" Now Boo was interested.

"Yes, the Sioux were fierce warriors, and even though the soldiers outnumbered them, they fought the Army to a standstill. Not until after the Battle of Little Big Horn did the United States government send so many soldiers to the frontier that they overwhelmed the tribes."

"Grandma, Isn't Little Big Horn where Crazy Horse killed General Custer and his troops?"

"Boo Bear, you know your history, but the battle wasn't the end of the story. After their defeat, the government confined almost all the Indians on reservations. Rations and supplies guaranteed by the treaty were poor quality … if they arrived at all. A lot of the government agents were crooks who stole from the tribes."

Grandma paused for a moment and then went on. "By 1890 a major revolt was brewing among the Indians. A Paiute Indian named Wovoka, who claimed he was the messiah come to prepare the Indians for their salvation, started a movement called the Ghost Dance. Tribes all over the country came to Nevada to meet with Wovoka and learn the Ghost Dance. Wovoka claimed the earth would soon perish and then come alive again, and all the Indians would live there forever, free from suffering in a wonderful garden."

"Wow, Grandma, that sounds a little like Christianity."

Grandma nodded in agreement. "Wovoka got a lot of his ideas from the Bible, but he added in some of his own. He was very strict about living at peace with everyone and being honest in all your dealings. He warned about following the ways of the whites and cautioned against drinking alcohol, which he called 'the destroyer.' His followers believed if they exhausted themselves dancing the Ghost Dance, they could have a kind of death experience and glimpse the 'paradise to come,' filled with their ancestors."

The story fascinated Boo. "But how did the Ghost Dance come to Petaluma?"

"This is where our family comes in, honey. In early October 1890, Kicking Bear, a great Sioux warrior, visited Chief Sitting Bull in Dakota. He told him great numbers of Indians were followers of the new religion. But Kicking Bear lied to Sitting Bull. Instead of telling the chief about Wovoka's desire to live peacefully with all people, he tried to use the new religion to instigate a revolt against the whites. He got Sitting Bull to go on the warpath and showed him special Ghost Dance shirts, which he claimed would protect the Indians against the white man's bullets.

"When the American government heard about Sitting Bull's involvement, they immediately sent troops to arrest Sitting Bull and to bring the uprising to a close. The American troops, still angry about their defeat at the Little Big Horn, murdered Sitting Bull and instigated the terrible massacre at Wounded Knee. Some survivors fled to Nevada and California. One, a war chief named Red Bull, came to Petaluma with his wife and daughter, hoping General Vallejo would protect him, but General Vallejo had died a year earlier, and they felt helpless. They were ready to give up hope when they met a local rancher, John Jamison, who was sympathetic to Red Bull. He invited the chief to stay at his ranch.

"John Jamison, your Great-Great-Grandfather, fell in love with the chief's daughter and married her in 1893. When the US Army found out Red Bull was hiding out on the ranch, they came to arrest him. Jamison warned Red Bull, and he fled. The authorities didn't bother your Great-Great-Grandmother Jamison, because her husband was an influential local man, but they captured Red Bull in Ukiah and sent him back to the Dakotas where they hanged him in 1895.

"Ever since then, they've called this place Ghost Dancer Ranch. The locals even say on the night of the full moon, the ghost of old Red Bull still dances the Ghost Dance out in the caves on the back part of the ranch, but that's just ignorance gone to seed.

"As for how you got here, John Jamison and his wife had one son, your Great-Grandfather, Alton Jamison, my father. Then I was born, and when I grew up, I married your Grandpa Roberts. Your dad came along, and when he grew up, he got married. Them you were born, and now here we are."

Boo looked up at her grandmother. "Wow, Grandma, how come I never heard this story before?"

"You know, your dad never seemed to be too interested in the ranch's history. He didn't like farm life much, and as soon as he could, he left here to pursue a career in business. When your Aunt Sharon married Bob Masters and moved to Marin County, she didn't seem interested in the ranch anymore. You're the first one of my grandkids I've told the story to."

Grandma glanced at the clock above the desk. "Oh, goodness, look at the time! I've got chores to do now, Boo. Why don't you stay here and read some of these clippings?" She grabbed an old sweater off the coat rack and left Boo alone in the office.

Boo sat quietly, pondering everything Grandma told her. *Whew. I can't wait to share this story with Jacie.*

Deep in the dark cave, two voices whispered together.

"We must awaken the others, for the time has come."

"Yes, but we must be careful, for the enemy will send his warriors to help the child."

"Yes, careful, careful, we must be very careful. Let the drum sound to awaken those who sleep, for we must be strong and walk in the Dark One's strength."

"Let us dance then …"

# CHAPTER TWO
## THE SECRET IN THE CLOCK

Boo sat at Grandma's desk and looked at the things spread out before her—some faded pictures, the newspaper articles she read, and some miscellaneous pieces of paper. One picture was of a tall, handsome Indian man in full war dress with an eagle-feather headdress and leather fringed jacket. The caption on the back said *Red Bull, 1889.* Boo stared at the photo. *So, he's my Great-Great-Great-Grandfather!*

She pulled out another picture of a tall man with dark hair and a full beard. He wore a dark suit and had intense eyes looking straight into the camera. Beside him stood a lovely Indian girl in a white beaded buckskin dress. Boo looked at the back—*John and Ruth Jamison, wedding day, 1893.*

*She's beautiful, and he's so intense looking.*

Reaching into the box once more, Boo lifted the few remaining pieces of paper and saw something lying in the bottom—a strange-looking key with a large circle of metal at the end of the shaft. A piece of white cotton muslin cloth embellished with feathers and painted symbols was fastened to the circle with a leather thong. In the middle of the cloth was an embroidered picture of an eagle in flight. The colors were still bright, and the bird almost looked alive. She set the cloth down and examined the key in the light.

*What is all this? And what does the key unlock?*

Boo set the strange key aside on the desk and looked through the papers once more. She read about the arrest and subsequent execution of Red Bull for taking part in the uprising at Wounded Knee Creek in South Dakota in 1890. One article was full of very biased statements about the "evil and mysterious" Ghost Dance rebellion and the messianic leader, Wovoka.

The other stories told about Sitting Bull's warriors killing the brave soldiers of Custer's command and the great Army victory at Wounded Knee following those killings. The articles were dated 1893. Boo stacked all the materials and placed them back into the box. "Now things are getting interesting," she said to herself. "I can't wait until Jacie gets here. Oh boy, a haunted ranch. Maybe this summer won't be as boring as I thought."

Getting up from the desk, she decided she should do a little exploring before she read the rest of the clippings. The old house was the kind an inquisitive teenager would choose for an adventure, although Boo sometimes let her snooping get the best of her.

Before she left for California, and after a sleuthing adventure, Boo's mom sat her down. "I won't say curiosity killed the cat applies in your case, but you need to be careful, sweetie. If you keep digging at everything, one of these days, you'll uncover something a little too much for you to handle."

Boo had laughed. "Oh, Mom, you worry too much."

Mom shook her head and smiled. "Boo, your father and I worry about your amazing ability to get into messes we need to help resolve. And your Grandma doesn't know you as well as I do."

Boo thought about the discussion with her mom and smiled.

*What could happen at my Grandparents' house?*

She decided she'd start at the top of the house and work her way down. Picking up a flashlight from Grandpa's workbench on the back porch, she went upstairs and poked around until she came to the door leading to the attic. She cautiously opened the door.

The stairs led up to the left, and the walls were made of unfinished boards. She felt for a light switch but couldn't find one, so she switched on the flashlight and climbed until she reached the top. A large room stretched away into the shadows. The attic was dark and still.

She stepped into the room. Piles of boxes leaned against the walls, and various pieces of furniture covered with sheets and stacks of other dust-covered items filled the room. Boo walked across the bare wooden floor, her steps echoing in the dark. At the back of the big room was a doorway leading into a long hall. She ambled down the hall, shining the light here and there. Black and white photos of the ranch and portraits of people in old-fashioned clothes hung on the walls. Several rooms opened off the hallway with more stuff piled in them. Trunks with colorful stickers on them and tall wardrobes stood against the walls.

At the end of the hall was a closed door. She had a hard time turning the knob, but at last, the door swung open with a creaking noise, and she stepped inside.

The room was large but plain, with short walls and an angled ceiling on both sides sloping up toward the center of the roof. A large brass bed frame stood against one wall next to a chest of drawers with a mirror mounted on top. Two plain wooden chairs stood stacked in a corner.

Straight ahead, a huge grandfather clock at least seven feet tall and about three feet across stood against the back wall. Wooden shelves filled with books covered the whole wall on either side of the clock. The clock had stopped at six o'clock. Dust covered the glass face, and the numerals were an old-fashioned Gothic style. The front of the clock contained a glass door through which Boo could see the clockworks hanging down. She pulled the wooden knob, and the door swung open to disclose a closet-like space. A large key meant for winding the clock hung on a hook.

"What a strange place for such a big clock." Her words echoed in the spooky quietness of the attic.

She looked for a place to wind the clock. The face was in a section at the top behind a little glass door with a knob. A slot was visible below the hands, so she pulled the small door open and inserted the key. It fit! As she wound the clock, the spring tightened, and the gears of the clock moved with an audible ticking sound. When finished, she hung the key back on the hook. The soft tick-tock was the only sound in the eerie quiet.

Then she shined the light into the space one more time. The beam picked up something in the back wall of the clock. Boo pushed aside the weights and discovered a small hole the same shape as the one she had put the key in to wind the clock. She pushed the key into the hole, but the mechanism was stiff and wouldn't turn. She tried again but nothing happened. She turned the key harder, and suddenly, with a loud click, the back wall of the clock moved!

She pulled out the key and then pushed on the back of the clock. The panel swung open like a door out into darkness. She crawled forward and shined the flashlight into the hole. In front of her was an empty space, and across from her was a rock wall with a ladder bolted to the stones.

Leaning into the space, she shined the light up and down and discovered a two-foot wide gap between the wooden wall of the room and the rock wall where the ladder hung. The space stretched from the roof downward and disappeared into the darkness. The musty smell from the shaft almost choked her. Then, from far below, she heard the muffled sound of a drum. Deep, slow, beats echoed up the dark passageway, grim and foreboding, and a chill ran down Boo's spine.

On the hill behind the ranch, a lone figure moved up a small canyon. The mist and rain had turned the trail into a muddy mess, but the figure left no footprints. A poncho on the figure's shoulders warded off the rain, and a large black hat hid the face.

Slipping up the trail, the mysterious figure came to a thick stand of manzanita scrub. Turning uphill, the silent figure stepped into a small gap in the brush and disappeared.

# CHAPTER THREE
## DRUMS IN THE DARK

Jacie Masters lay on her bed feeling crabby. Her mother had just informed her she was going to spend two weeks with her grandparents at their ranch in Petaluma with her cousin, Hannah, from Michigan, whom she'd never met. How could her mother do this to her? She could have at least given her warning. This whole thing was awful and cut the heart out of the whole summer!

"I don't want to go to Petaluma," she said out loud in her whiniest voice.

"But you are, Punkin," her mother said through the door. "It's already decided. Now, may I come in, sweetie? I need to talk to you."

"No!" Jacie flipped over on her face.

"Jacie Elizabeth, I want to talk to you!"

Jacie recognized her tone. "Okay."

Her mom came into the room and sat down on the bed next to her. "The way you're acting is not acceptable, honey. I know you're disappointed, but your cousin, Hannah, really needs someone right now. Her mom and dad are in Texas looking for a new house, and she's all by herself out at the ranch."

"But, Mom," Jacie whined, turned over, and looked up at her mom. "Nicole and I had the whole summer planned. You know, go to the mall every day, hang out, go to the pool—stuff like that."

"Well, I hate to disappoint you, but you girls are only thirteen years old. I don't think I would let you spend all your time unsupervised at the mall. You're growing up, but you're not grown up yet." Her mother frowned. "Besides, your dad and I have to go to a pastors' convention, and this solves the problem of where you'll stay while we're gone. Bobby and Trinity will stay with Grandma Masters, and you will be with Hannah—much more fun than being with a bunch of boring pastors."

"But I don't even know Hannah, Mom." The anguish returned to Jacie's voice. "What if she's a total geek?"

"From what I hear from Aunt Carol, Hannah is a great girl, smart and fun-loving. I think you'll get on well with her." She smiled.

"But what about Nicole? She's my best friend."

"Punkin, Nicole will get through the two weeks you're gone, and then you'll have the rest of the summer and next year at school to be together. So, just buck up and do what your dad and I are asking. You know you love Grandma and Grandpa Roberts, and you love going to the ranch."

Jacie sighed. "I wish I could decide for myself what I want to do. But I'll go." She let her shoulders slump as she resigned herself to her fate. "I can't promise I'll be her best bud, but I'll try to be nice. I mean, at least I can take my cell phone and talk to Nicole as much as I want to help me pass the time."

"Punkin, I don't want you to be on the phone all the time. You can take your cell phone, and you can call Nicole once a day, but you can't talk longer than fifteen minutes. Your dad and I can't afford a huge bill, and besides, I want you to focus your attention on Hannah. We gave you a phone so you could stay in touch with us, not to be the center of your existence. And no texting. I want you to get out and enjoy your grandparent's ranch—such a beautiful old place—and there are lots of things to do besides being glued to your cell phone."

Her mom got up to leave.

Jacie waited until she left and then muttered to herself, "Oh brother, now I can't even use my phone when I want. This will be the worst summer ever." She lay on her bed feeling sorry for herself.

Boo knelt inside the old clock and listened to the sound of the drum floating up the dark passage. Something mournful and dark resonated from the slow beat. The sound faded in and out as if coming from a long way off.

"Now, this is scary. Grandma said old Red Bull's ghost still hung around the ranch, but I don't believe in ghosts. There's got to be an explanation."

Her curiosity overcame her fear, and she stuck her head and arm through the opening into the gap between the walls. In the beam from her flashlight, she saw the ladder was old and bolted to the stones opposite her with metal brackets.

She remembered how Grandpa told her the stone wall was the back part of the house. They must have built these wooden walls with a space between them and the stone wall so there would be a secret passage. But why? Gathering her courage, she reached across the short expanse, took hold of the top rung, and swung onto the ladder. She took a cautious look to make sure there were no spider webs. Yuck! Of all the things in the world, spiders were the worst.

Keeping the light pointed into the darkness below, she made her way down the ladder. The passage was close and dark, but she could feel cool air flowing up from somewhere. After she descended several steps, her foot couldn't find the next rung. She shined the light into the blackness and discovered she was on the last rung with nothing but a dark hole below. In the flashlight's beam, she could barely see the bottom of the shaft below her.

She hung on the ladder and shined the light all around but couldn't see any openings. Halfway down, Boo found newer brickwork filling part of the space between the wall and the old stones. The new bricks went all the way to the bottom of the shaft, and the ladder went down beside them.

*This must be where Grandpa Jamison attached the big fireplace in the dining room to the original one in the old wall.*

Boo could go no further, and if she jumped down to look for another door, she could never get back up.

Boo could still hear the drum, a little louder now, and in the darkness low voices sang words she couldn't understand. Her courage evaporated, and she climbed back up the ladder as fast as she could.

When she got to the top, she leaned across, grabbed the edge of the opening, and pulled herself back into the clock. In her haste, she scrambled through the opening, knocking the flashlight out of her hand. It disappeared down into the darkness, bouncing off the walls. The flashlight landed at the bottom with a loud thump, and the beam went dark. The drumming ceased, and now the shaft was shrouded in darkness once again.

Boo closed the door to the secret passage and scooted through the clock. She climbed out and closed the glass door behind her.

She took a minute to catch her breath, and then she remembered she'd dropped the flashlight. "Oh pancakes! I've lost the flashlight, and I scared the ghost." She stood staring at the clock. "There must be a way into the passage from down below. I've got to get Grandpa's flashlight back."

She made her way out of the clock room and down the long hall to the stairway, determined to solve the mystery of the drums.

Boo said nothing to Grandma or Grandpa and went to bed feeling a little scared but excited about what she discovered.

During the night, she had strange dreams. Indian warriors chased her through long tunnels and secret passages, and while she ran, the beating drum never ceased.

The sun had gone down over the western hills many hours before. Behind the barn, a dark figure stood watching as the lights turned off one by one in the big house on the knoll. A slim moon appeared in the sky, and dark clouds scudded past. The light from the moon cast spectral shadows on the side of the old house. The figure watched for a little while longer, and then turned and disappeared around the side of the barn into the growing darkness, leaving the imprint of boot heels with a distinctive shape in the mud.

# CHAPTER FOUR
## THE MYSTERY DEEPENS

The sun poured in through Boo's window when she awoke the next morning. Bright rays sliced through the dust motes in the air, and she could hear a horse whinnying outside.

"Oh boy, sun at last," she almost shouted as she jumped from the bed then scrounged through her drawer until she found the summer shorts Mom bought her as a going-away present. She slipped on her favorite top, scooted into the bathroom to wash up, and then headed down the back stairs to the kitchen. She grabbed the railings on both sides of the stairs, swung over the last two steps, and crashed right into a blonde girl walking past the door at the bottom of the stairs with a bowl of cereal in her hands.

The two of them went sprawling on the floor, and Cheerios and milk went everywhere. Because of their position, almost on top of each other, Boo got a good look at the girl. Her hair was shoulder length, and she was skinny, cute, and overdressed in a red shirt and matching short pants. And now, she was also wearing Cheerios.

The girl's face turned red. "Why don't you look where you're going? You've ruined my outfit."

Boo looked down at her.

*Oh pancakes. This has got to be Jacie.*

She wanted to say how sorry she was until she noticed a single Cheerio right on the end of the girl's nose. Instead of an apology, what came out was a chuckle, and then, though she tried to stop, a laugh. Boo cracked up. She laughed out loud, and Jacie's face grew redder and redder.

The kitchen door flew open, and Grandma and another woman burst in. Grandma stopped and took in the scene before her. "Good grief, girls, what happened?"

"She came flying out of the stairwell and crashed me over," Jacie sputtered in anger. "She's ruined my outfit, and all she can do is laugh."

Boo tried to stop laughing. "I'm very sorry ..." She tried to choke out an apology. "But she has a Cheerio on the end of her nose."

Grandma and Aunt Sharon looked at Jacie, and both of them chuckled too.

"Great! This geek almost kills me, ruins my outfit, and laughs at me, and all you can do is laugh too. Great!" Jacie stood, and with tears in her eyes, she stormed out of the room.

Boo watched her cousin disappear upstairs. She turned to the two adults. "That went well, don't ya think?" Then she jumped up from her seat in the middle of the kitchen floor and grabbed her aunt's hand.

"Gee, Aunt Sharon, I'm so sorry. I didn't mean to knock her down. I didn't even know you guys were here."

Jacie's mom, Sharon Masters, looked at Boo for a moment and then smiled and pulled Boo into a great big hug. "I know you didn't mean to crash into Punkin, sweetie," and then she held Boo at arm's length. "My goodness, Mom, look how she's grown. Boo, I haven't seen you since you were three years old." She smiled through the tears in her eyes. "You look just like my brother, John." She hugged Boo again.

"Punkin will calm down, Boo. She's had some of her plans changed—plans she made without asking me—and she's having a little trouble with being here. I'm sure you two will get along great as soon as she gets to know you better."

"Grab yourself some cereal, and sit down and eat, girl." Grandma grabbed a rag and finished wiping up the mess.

"Grandma, I think I should go apologize to Jacie before I eat." And she went off to make amends. She went to the door of Jacie's room and knocked.

"Who is it?" Her cousin's voice sounded muffled.

Boo took a deep breath. "It's me, Jacie, can I come in?"

"Right, what do you want to do, finish the job?"

"No." Boo opened the door a crack and peeked in. "I came to apologize. I didn't mean to knock you down. I've been so looking forward to meeting you, and now I guess I've spoiled everything. Please forgive me. Can't I come in?"

"Okay, I guess." Jacie rolled away from Boo and faced the window.

She stepped into the room and sat on the edge of the bed. "Now, look. I'm sorry. I apologize. You can lie here and feel sorry for yourself, or you can accept my apology and get a grip." She used her best take-charge voice. "I want to start over. Please. I've wanted to meet you forever, and I know we can be great friends. So, I'll go first."

Boo stood and put on a broad southern accent. "Why you must be mah cousin, Jacie Masters, from Californ-i-ay. Ah've been so wanting to meet y'all, and now heah you are."

Despite herself, her cousin's antics lightened Jacie's mood. And the put-on accent was hilarious. She rolled over and faced Boo. "Okay, I'll give you another chance, but I have to tell you, I had other plans for the next two weeks, so I'm cranky. If you promise not to knock me down again, I'll accept your apology."

"Done!" Her cousin stuck out her hand. "Hannah Elise Roberts, pleased ta meetcha. You can call me Boo."

Jacie was a little taken back by her outgoing cousin, but she took Boo's hand. "I'm Jacie Masters—Jacie Elizabeth Masters—but you can call me the Cheerios Kid."

They both laughed.

Boo talked a mile a minute. "I'm so glad you're here, Jacie. Like I said, I've wanted to meet you forever and—"

"Almost everybody calls me Punkin," Jacie interrupted. "So, you should too."

"Okay, I will. Anyway, I'm glad you're here because there's a mystery in this house we've got to solve."

Punkin's eyes went wide. "A mystery?"

Boo outlined what Grandma had told her about the Ghost Dancers and Red Bull, their great-great-grandfather. Then, lowering her voice, she said, "Yesterday, I found a secret passage from the attic down to the cellar. There's a ladder, but the ladder doesn't go all the way down, so I couldn't see if there was a door at the bottom."

"A secret passage? How exciting."

"Yeah, I know there's got to be a door into the passage from the cellar. I've got to get in there, because I dropped Grandpa's flashlight down there. Want to look with me?"

"Sure, have you told Grandma?"

Boo shook her head. "Well, I, uh, I haven't told Grandma yet because she might not let us do any more detective work. I thought we could do a little more investigating and let this be our secret for a while."

Punkin frowned. "Well, I don't know. There could be some danger."

"Oh, Punkin, we've just got to be careful. Come on, are you a scaredy-cat or what?"

Punkin rolled over and stood. "I'm no scaredy-cat! Let's see this secret passage."

"That's the spirit." Boo slapped Punkin on the back. "But we should wait until your mom's gone. And I want to show you the stuff Grandma showed me. Oh, in case you didn't notice, we're at a ranch. I would advise you to put on something more, uh, disposable?"

They laughed again.

"I tell you, Punkin, there's something strange going on around here." Boo's voice got mysterious as they went out the door. "Oh, and I forgot to tell you about the ghost ..."

Punkin grabbed Boo's arm. "What ghost?"

North of Petaluma, a black Lexus pulled into the parking lot at the Washoe House, a roadhouse and restaurant on Stony Point Road. Two men in dark suits and sunglasses got out, and one opened the back door to let another older man out of the car.

As they stood by the car, a pickup with two men pulled up. "Sorry we're late," the driver of the truck said.

The older man squinted at the new arrivals. "No problem, Chief. We've only been here a few minutes. Now, let's all go have one of those great burgers while you tell us all about the perfect spot you found for a casino."

And the five men went into the restaurant together.

The room was large, but there were no windows. The walls were made of rough-cut stones, and the floor was dirt. A bitter-smelling green smoke filled the air. In the middle of the room where the smoke was thickest, a dead tree branch decorated with strange clumps of feathers, bones, and animal skulls rose from a mound of debris. Ghostly figures began to form within the smoke, shuffling counterclockwise and side stepping around the tree while they chanted in low, horrible voices.

The tempo increased. Round and round the dancers went, transfixed by the drum beating in the dark shadows of the room.

They danced without rest, on and on, chanting and shuffling.

The voices whispered together, urging on the figures in the smoke. "Dance, dance, for you summon the Dark One, and we need his power for what is coming."

# CHAPTER FIVE
## IN THE CELLAR

Boo stood chewing at her fingernail while Punkin and her mom said their goodbyes. Then Aunt Sharon walked across the front porch and took Boo into her arms.

"You haven't said a word this morning, honey. I hope you and Punkin are getting along."

"Oh, Aunt Sharon, I'm sorry. I've just got something on my mind. And don't worry; Punkin and I are already friends."

Aunt Sharon laughed. "Well, from what your mom says, I'm sure you'll keep Punkin occupied while we're gone." She gave Boo a kiss and walked down the front steps to her car.

Just then, Grandma came boiling around the side of the house in her old pickup, a cloud of dust trailing along behind her. She got out and walked over to Sharon to hug her goodbye. Aunt Sharon climbed into her car, waved goodbye to the girls, and drove down the hill.

Grandma turned to Punkin and Boo. "I'll be back in a while. I've got to go into town and meet Grandpa. We're having lunch with some people." And off she went, which created a perfect opportunity for the girls to go exploring.

Boo ran inside and dug through Grandpa's stuff on the back porch until she found two more flashlights, then went out on the front porch and handed one to Punkin. They went around to the side of the house. The only way into the cellar was through a sloped door coming out of the side of the house. Boo swung the panel up and open to reveal a set of stairs going down into the darkness. She paused and shined her light into the musty gloom then glanced at Punkin. Her cousin's face was a little pale.

"I don't know, Boo. It's kinda spooky down there."

Boo ignored her and started down the stairs. Punkin followed, a few steps behind. As they descended into the cellar, Boo explained about the secret passage. "I think the ladder goes down by the side of the big fireplace in the living room, so the entrance must be somewhere near the back of the house."

When they came to the bottom of the stairs, they stood there for a moment while their eyes adjusted to the darkness. A long hallway stretched out in front of them, with what looked like storage rooms and closets on either side. Dust-covered boxes, old furniture, and what looked like farm tools were stacked against the walls.

"Wow," Punkin breathed. "Grandma and Grandpa have sure collected a lot of stuff."

Boo shook her head. "A lot has probably been here way longer than they have. Come on, Punkin, let's check this place out." She pushed ahead with Punkin close behind.

They only went a little way when Boo stopped and pointed her flashlight at the floor. "Look, Punkin, someone's been down here." There in the dust were shoe prints pointing in the same direction they were heading.

Punkin pointed her light ahead. "And look there …" Long spider webs hung raggedly down from the large beams supporting the ceiling. "Someone brushed the cobwebs aside."

"You're right, Punkin," Boo said, nodding. "And these are boot prints—see, there's the heel and a gap and then the smooth bottom of the boot. The heel sure makes a funny mark. I wonder who was down here."

Punkin's hand shook, and the circle of light from her beam danced along the walls. "Oh, must have been Grandpa." Her voice squeaked a little, and she looked around to make sure no one else was there.

"Look, Punkin. There's a big door back there. Those boxes were stacked in front, but you can see by the marks someone moved them out of the way."

The girls pushed past the stacked boxes until they reached a heavy wooden door with a lever instead of a knob. Boo handed Punkin her light and pressed down on the lever.

"It's stuck, Punkin. Help me."

Punkin set the lights on a box and pushed on the lever with Boo. Finally, the lever moved, and the door creaked open. They grabbed up the lights and stepped through. Ahead of them was a large room with wooden walls. A structure made of bricks stuck out from against the back wall and went all the way up through the ceiling. In the front was a small metal door.

Boo inspected the bricks. "These are the same color as the bricks in the fireplace upstairs. I saw more like this when I was climbing down the ladder. This part must be what supports the fireplace and look ..." She bent down and opened the small door. A puff of white dust came out. "This is where you clean out the ashes that fall through the grate." She tapped on the wall on the right side of the brick structure. "There must be a space behind here where the ladder comes down next to the fireplace."

Punkin looked along the wall. "What do you think the secret ladder was for, Boo?"

"Grandma told me Great-Great-Grandpa Jamison hid old Red Bull here in the house for five years. I bet they built the passage so Red Bull could hide if anyone came around. He could just jump in from upstairs and get down to the cellar or hide in the passage. Find anything yet?"

"No, and this place is giving me the creeps." Punkin looked along the opposite wall for any sign of a door. She glanced up.

"Hey, Boo, look at this. Maybe there's a door behind this stuff."

Boo went over to where Punkin stood. A board with pegs sticking out was attached to the wall above them with several old coats, some ponchos, and some dungarees hanging on the pegs. As Punkin searched among the clothing for evidence of an opening, she stepped on a stack of boards, and they shifted under her. Her ankle twisted, and she grabbed hold of a coat to catch herself. As her weight pulled the peg down, a small square section of the wall slid to the left.

"Punkin, look!!"

The two of them stared at the small square opening. Boo shined her light in and stuck her head through.

"Good job, Punkin! And here's the ladder going all the way up. But the bottom rung is too high for me to reach."

The girls climbed into the shaft and looked up. The ladder perched about eight feet above the floor. Punkin stretched up but couldn't reach the rung. "I guess a tall man could jump up there and pull himself up."

Boo shrugged. "Well, we found the secret entrance, but this is not as mysterious as I thought … But what about the drum I heard? I'm sure the sound came from down here. We should go look at the stuff Grandma showed me. I still think there's more here than meets the eye."

Punkin looked at the small space. "I thought you said you dropped a flashlight down here."

"I did." Boo shined the light around the floor. but saw no flashlight. "Wait, look here." She bent down and picked up a piece of clear plastic. "This looks like a piece of the lens. The glass must have shattered when the flashlight landed. But where's the rest?"

At Essa's Restaurant in downtown Petaluma, Grandpa and Grandma Roberts sat in a booth in the back of the restaurant with two men from the Pomo Tribe at Cache Creek in a heated conversation.

Grandpa Roberts pointed his finger at the men and spoke loudly. "Ghost Dancer Ranch is not Native American land. The old place was homesteaded by a white rancher and has been in my wife's family since 1855."

"Yeah, but your wife's grandfather was an Indian, and we can use her heritage to our advantage." The younger of the two men interrupted the tirade. "We could get a Rancheria, no problem, and set up the casino right there. We have certain, shall we say, friends in high places."

"But when you bring gambling into a community," Grandma added, "the results are always bad. You'll destroy the culture of this town—of this whole area."

"You know what?" the older man said. "The white people came to our land two hundred years ago and didn't think twice about destroying our culture. Turnabout is fair play. And besides, we pass all the money on to the members of the tribe. Then they can make something of themselves."

Grandpa put his spoon in his coffee and stirred, clanking the edge of the cup. When he had everyone's attention, he started in. "Look here, you men. I may have been born at night, but I wasn't born last night. The Indians got the people of California to buy into the whole gaming scheme by convincing them the casinos would be out on a reservation in the boondocks. Now you guys are casino shopping in every town. This is a bait-and-switch scam. And besides, where does the money come from to buy the land to build this place?" Grandpa didn't wait for an answer. "It comes from the same crooks who run the casinos in Las Vegas. Don't give me your hogwash about the benevolent Tribal Council. You guys are in league with the devil, and you're only in this deal for the bucks."

"Look, Mr. Roberts, I don't want to fight with you." The young man tried to placate Grandpa. "The Miwoks in Graton are ready to put in a casino in Rohnert Park. Why should they get all the money? Gambling is coming to more California cities every day. Better you sell us your land at an incredible profit and get rich. There will be a casino here, and there's nothing you can do to stop us. We're offering you seven million dollars for your land. With your wife as a trustee of our corporation, and the history of this land's association with Indians, we can beat the Miwoks to the punch and put in our casino."

Grandpa frowned. "You boys just don't hear so good. The land is not for sale."

Grandma put her hand on Grandpa's arm. "We are Christians, and we don't believe in gambling because of the evil effect on cities and people. So, we're not interested in your proposal, no matter how much money you offer. We have all we need and a good life. The Lord is our security, not money. I don't need to say any more. Nice to meet you gentlemen, but we have things to do. Good day."

And with that, the Roberts's picked up the bill and headed for the cashier.

The two men watched as the elderly couple left the restaurant. The younger man scowled. "Jimmy ain't gonna like this."

His friend stared after the retreating couple. "Don't worry, Weasel. We'll do whatever we have to, but we're gonna get the old lady's land."

After Punkin and Boo left the cellar, they went back inside to go through the pile of pictures and articles in Grandma's box.

The strange key with the piece of cloth attached interested Boo, but when she'd asked, Grandma had said, "I'm not sure about the key. I found all this in my father's effects when he passed away, along with all the articles and receipts. I didn't throw anything away because of the sentimental value." Grandma grinned. "I'm just an old packrat."

The articles and the miscellaneous pieces of paper in the box's bottom drew Boo's attention. She looked at some random numbers scrawled on one scrap then handed them to Punkin.

"What do you make of this, Punkin?"

Punkin took the scraps and studied them for a few minutes. Finally, she looked up. "How many steps were on the ladder to nowhere, Boo?"

"About twenty. You could see from the bottom of the shaft the ladder came down to about eight feet above the floor. A tall man could come in from the bottom and jump up to the ladder."

"You know what, Boo? I'm sure Great-Great-Grandfather Jamison built the passage so Red Bull had a place to hide if anybody came looking for him."

Boo nodded. "Sure he did. I believe you're right. You know, you're not as dumb as your city-girl outfit made you look."

Punkin flashed a look in Boo's direction. "Leave my outfit out of this. I earned the money from a lot of babysitting, and I like the color a lot."

"Okay, okay, just kidding. Grandma can make the outfit look as good as new I bet. Anyway, why did you ask about the ladder?"

Punkin held up the scrap of paper she'd been examining. "Well, look at this—one of the pieces of paper in the box has a lot of numbers written down."

Boo looked at the numbers on the wrinkled piece of paper while Punkin talked. "From what I've read about secret passages, a lot of times there's a secret in the secret. I mean, what if there's another way out of the passage, a way Grandpa Jamison wanted to keep hidden? Look, the first number says LR13; the second says 3SR; then U2S; then P; then HOTL. What if LR13 means something about the 13th rung of the ladder?"

"Yeah, I get your drift." Boo smiled at her cousin. "It's on a stone wall so 3SR might be something about the third stone to the right. You're right, Punkin! These are directions written in code! First thing in the morning we'll go have a look." Boo put her arm around Punkin's shoulder. "Hey, Cousin, you may have just solved the mystery."

The black Lexus pulled up next to the truck in the underground parking lot in Santa Rosa. The back window rolled down, and a well-dressed older man stared at them and then flicked a cigar ash out on their feet. "Well, Chief, how did you do?"

"They didn't buy the proposal, Jimmy."

The well-dressed man leaned back in the seat. "Well, too bad— that's just too bad." The window rolled up silently as the car sped away.

A silent figure had watched from a vantage point on the hill behind the ranch as the two girls came up out of the cellar and went around to the front of the house. His intense eyes, hidden by an old black hat, fixed on them until they went inside.

Then the mysterious stranger turned and disappeared into the eucalyptus grove behind the barn. His brown, calloused hand clutched the flashlight with the broken lens, but his moccasined feet left no mark on the trail.

# CHAPTER SIX
## THE SECRET OF THE LADDER

Punkin and Boo stood in front of the clock in the attic room. Boo opened the door of the clock and took the key off the hook. She pushed the weights aside, reached in, and unlocked the secret door in the back.

Punkin looked over Boo's shoulder. "How did you ever find the keyhole?"

Boo shrugged. "Kind of the same way you found the peg downstairs—by accident." She crawled inside the clock and stuck her head into the opening. "Okay, Punkin, I'll climb down the ladder. Oh, give me the extra flashlight first. Now, when I get down, you read me the directions." She leaned into the shaft and clambered onto the ladder.

Punkin held the flashlight steady. "Go down to the thirteenth rung."

Boo put the small flashlight in her back pocket and climbed down, counting as she went. "Okay, I'm there."

"The next notation says 3SR. Count over three stones to your right."

Boo reached out and felt the wall. Finding the third stone to the right was difficult among the uneven stones, but she found one smoother than the rest.

"Okay, what next, Punkin?"

"It says U2S and then P. Count up to the second stone and try pulling."

Boo moved her hand up and found another stone much smoother than the surrounding stones. She tried pulling but couldn't find a place to grip. The ladder shifted under her.

"Nothing's happening, Punkin, but this part of the ladder swung a little."

"Be careful then and try pushing on the rock."

Boo pushed hard, and the stone depressed into the wall. The section of the wall directly in front of her pivoted silently into the great rock chimney and the section of the ladder she was standing on separated from the top part and swung into the wall. She heard a rattling sound like chains dragging, and the ladder slid down the wall about ten feet and came to a jarring stop.

Boo's feet bounced off the ladder rung, and she lost her grip. She fell backward into the darkness.

The smoke from the sacred fire drifted up between the two men. The older one, dressed in the ceremonial garb of a Paiute medicine man, lifted the pot of burning herbs and wafted the smoke in four directions. "There are four sacred herbs in the native culture," he said in a low voice. "Sage purifies a room of negative energies. Sweet grass brings in the spirit to heal you. Cedar is for purification and creating an atmosphere in which the spirits can work. There's a sweetness they like that's attractive to the energies of the invisible world. Tobacco has always been sacred for ceremonies of smoking the pipe to bless the earth."

The old man breathed in and used his hands to move the smoke toward the younger man, who breathed in deeply. "Now we have prepared ourselves, I will tell you about the calling on your life."

The young man nodded at the words.

The medicine man went on. "Wovoka, the messiah, had a great vision during the solar eclipse on January 1, 1889. Wovoka's vision revealed the resurrection of the Paiute dead and the removal of whites and their works from North America. To bring this vision to pass, Wovoka taught us to live an upstanding life and perform what he called the Ghost Dance. While performing the Ghost Dance, we could visit relatives who had left their bodies. Because so many of the people had lost friends and relatives in war, this part of the ceremony was healing. The Lakota, Cheyenne, and Arapaho expanded the meaning further after being told in dreams that wearing certain designs on clothing would protect them in battle.

"The Ghost Dance unified Native American people, even tribes with a tradition of conflict. Their strength frightened government officials, who feared the Arapahos, Cheyenne, and Sioux would come together as they did when they defeated General Custer at Little Big Horn. Most Ghost Dancers did not embrace warlike behavior. But the Sioux insisted we were to revolt against the white man with war and wear the shirts would protect us in battle.

"Wovoka told Kicking Bear, the Sioux war chief, he was wrong, but the Miniconjou and the Lakota insisted on taking the warpath. Even though most Ghost Dancers did not follow Kicking Bear, the government gunned down Ghost Dancers at Wounded Knee during a peaceful ceremony. The soldiers shot women and children in the back as they were trying to escape. Many say this was in retaliation for Custer's death at the Little Big Horn, since the perpetrators of the massacre were the Seventh Cavalry.

"Now, one hundred years later, the native people are seeking their messiah again. Many feel the time of the resurrection is at hand, and they want to follow Wovoka's vision and dance the Ghost Dance once more. But there are still those who would take the warpath. When the war chief, Red Bull, came to California after Wounded Knee, he brought with him a Ghost Dancer shirt Wovoka gave him. When they captured him, they did not find the shirt. Red Bull went to his grave insisting he had renounced the warpath and had found the true way. You must find the shirt of Red Bull. I know Red Bull did not have the shirt when they captured him, so he must have left the garment at the ranch. When you have the Ghost Dancer shirt, you will take your place as leader of the path of peace. Only you can do this, for you are the great-great-grandson of Wovoka, and the people will follow you."

The young man nodded. "Yes, Grandfather, I will find the shirt, and help my people find the way of peace."

When Boo disappeared, Punkin was scared out of her wits. "Boo!" she called but got no answer. She looked into the shaft, but all she could see was a smooth wall right where Boo had been standing. "Boo! Are you all right?"

She was about to run downstairs to find Grandma when she heard a slight rumbling sound. When she looked back in the shaft, the ladder was back but no Boo. Then the wall pivoted again, and a light came up the shaft out of the opening.

"I'm okay, Punkin," Boo called up to her. "I got the wind knocked out of me. Watch this!"

The wall rumbled and pivoted back, revealing Boo hanging on the ladder, grinning.

"Now I know what HOTL meant. Hang on to the ladder. When the wall pivoted, the ladder just slid down the wall and dropped me into another passage. There's a chain that comes out of the wall; it's hooked to the ladder. I only fell about three feet, but I landed flat on my back on top of a big rock. If I had held on, I could've have jumped right down after the ladder stopped."

"How did you get out?"

Boo climbed up the ladder. "I looked around for a flat stone like the one I pressed out here. Then I found one set right in the wall, and when you push, the ladder slides back up and pivots back out here. When you push again, the ladder pivots into the wall and slides down. There's another passage down on the other side of the big rock below the ladder. There are handholds cut in the rock to get down to the passage,"

Punkin backed out of the clock and Boo climbed through.

"The tunnel goes down into the hill, Punkin. I bet this place was already here before Great-Great-Great Grandpa Jamison built the ranch house. He must have discovered the swinging wall and left the secret code in the box. I bet he used these passages as Red Bull's real hiding place. We need to get down there and see where they lead."

"Gee, Boo, who would've thought there were so many secrets around this old place? When should we go?"

Boo closed the front door of the clock. "Well, I think we need to do a little research first. Did you bring your laptop?"

"Yes, and my Dad got me a wireless card so I could log onto the internet."

Boo smiled. "Great! We need to find out more about the Ghost Dancers." Suddenly, she stopped. "Do you hear something?"

Punkin nodded with wide eyes. Boo opened the clock. From somewhere underneath them, and yet far away, came the sound of a solitary drum.

The three men in the black Lexus sped along Highway101 toward Ukiah. The well-dressed man muttered, "So, the old man doesn't want to sell." He leaned forward and spoke to two dangerous-looking men in the front seat. "Boys, if the old man won't listen, then maybe someone should get him out of the way so we can deal with his wife. She's part Indian."

The man who wasn't driving turned around. "How should we handle this, Jimmy?"

"Well, Pete, maybe he should have an accident or something. I'll leave the details up to you and Artie. That's what I pay you for."

"Yeah, Boss. That's what you pay us for." Pete patted the bulge in his coat.

Grandpa Roberts looked the stranger over. "Who exactly recommended you?"

"Bob Peterson, the rancher from Cloverdale who sells you sheep," the young man with intense eyes answered.

"Right, Bob Peterson. Tell me your name again."

"My name's Jack Wilson, and I'm from Nevada. I can do every kind of ranch work, and in case you're interested, I'm a full-blooded Paiute Indian." The young man smiled.

"Well, Jack, I am short one hand. My best horse wrangler took off with his gal from Sebastopol to get married, and I don't expect he'll be back for a while. Okay, I'll try you out. The pay is two hundred dollars a week with room and board and Sundays off. If that works for you, you can put your gear in the bunkhouse."

"Fine with me, sir. You won't regret this."

"Well, I'll check with Peterson, and if he okays you, you can stay. Now get your stuff moved in, but don't unpack until I call Bob." Grandpa headed up to the house.

# CHAPTER SEVEN
## DANGER ON THE ROAD

Grandpa Roberts drove along the fire road up above the ranch looking for some stray sheep. He made this drive almost every day to keep an eye on things.

The view from up in the canyon was some of the prettiest land he'd ever seen, and the ranch stretched out below him. In front of him was the first ridge of the coastal hills. If he scanned the ridge, he could see the gap where the Petaluma River flowed down toward San Francisco Bay. Across the bay, almost seventy miles away, he could see Mount Diablo.

Suddenly, he heard a rumble and crashing sounds on the hillside above him. He looked up in time to see a huge boulder thundering down directly toward him. He jammed down the accelerator but a second too late. The boulder smashed into his truck and knocked Grandpa sideways toward the edge of the road. The wheels went over the bank.

Grandpa Roberts lost control, and the old truck slipped over the edge. Next thing he knew, he was flung onto his side, and he held his breath as the truck slid down into the canyon. He went down about sixty feet and the truck banged up against a big pine, jolting Grandpa's shoulder against the door. The truck flipped over and slid around, pointing uphill. The doors flew open.

Grandpa Roberts shook his head and looked around. He was hanging upside down in his seat belt and his head hurt. His arm was throbbing and felt broken. "Whoa! Where did that rock come from?"

As he fumbled for the belt buckle, he heard crashing in the bushes uphill from him and then two male voices. Someone was coming downhill toward the truck.

"Come on, Artie, get down there and make sure he's dead," one voice said.

"I'm going, Pete," the other man responded, "but I don't think he could have lived through rolling down the hill."

"If he's not dead, use a rock or something and finish him, but make sure he looks like he died in the crash."

Grandpa got the seat belt buckle undone and dropped onto the ceiling of the truck. He suppressed a yell of agony as he landed on his broken arm. The pain of the drop and the shock of the crash took effect, and he felt himself passing out.

Then, to his surprise, strong brown arms reached in and pulled him from the truck. Someone whispered in his ear. "Be quiet." As the darkness closed in on him, he felt himself being lifted like a baby and carried away.

The sound of the drum came drifting up the shaft. Punkin and Boo froze.

"It's Red Bull's ghost!" Punkin squeaked. "He's doing the Ghost Dance, and he's coming after us."

Boo grabbed her cousin, who was shaking like a wet puppy. "I don't believe in ghosts, Punkin," she whispered. "Now be quiet, or you'll attract the ghost's attention."

Punkin held on to Boo. "Wh … what should we do?"

The drum was real, and Boo wasn't too sure of herself. "Well, I don't want to go searching the tunnel by myself. There's something strange going on here, but I think we need to ask Grandpa to help us." Then the faint sound of the drum ceased.

"I sure don't want to go looking for the ghost either, unless we have help."

"Come on." Boo grabbed Punkin's arm. "Let's find Grandpa."

They ran to the door, but when they pulled it open, they crashed into their grandmother.

"Oh, hi, Grandma." Boo tried to act nonchalant as they untangled themselves. "Uh, we were just exploring in the attic and found a secret passageway in the clock …"

Grandma hushed Boo with a stern look. "Never mind that now, Boo. I need your help. Your grandpa is missing."

Boo froze. "Grandpa missing? But how, when …?"

Pete and Artie pushed through the brush to where the truck lay against the tree. Both doors hung open.

Pete pointed to the truck. "Get over there and see if he rolled out."

Artie ran around the truck and looked inside the cab. "Pete, he's gone!"

"What?"

Pete looked in the other side. A smear of fresh blood clung to the window, and the driver's seatbelt was unbuckled. When he didn't see Grandpa, Pete pointed to the woods. "Well, don't just stand there, Artie. We've got to find him."

Both men searched among the trees and under the bushes, but they couldn't find Grandpa Roberts.

# The Mystery of Ghost Dancer Ranch

A dark figure with a hat pulled low carried an unconscious Grandpa Roberts through the manzanita until they came to a thick clump of scrub. Pushing through, the figure ducked down and stepped sideways into a dark opening in the hillside, and they disappeared as though they had never been there.

# CHAPTER EIGHT
## MISSING!

Jack Wilson crept quietly through the cellar under the old farmhouse. Although late afternoon, the place was pitch dark, and he used his flashlight to follow the tracks of the two girls toward the stone wall at the back of the musty room.

His flashlight picked out another set of tracks the girls' sneakers had disturbed—his.

*I should have been more careful when I came down here last night.*

He hoped the girls weren't looking for the same thing he was.

*I've got to find Red Bull's Ghost Dancer shirt. It's a good thing old Roberts hired me. I couldn't go on sneaking around this place without getting found out.*

A movement had been growing in the local tribes to return to the ways of the Ghost Dance, and for Jack to take his place as the leader was critical. He was already active in the Bole Maru, the spiritual resistance movement helping bring back from the brink of extermination Northern California Indian tribes such as the Southern Pomo and the Coastal Miwoks. But now he was watching his brothers and sisters lose their spiritual focus as the lure of quick money from building casinos drew them away from their newfound spiritual beliefs.

If he could find Red Bull's shirt, he would be established as a leader among leaders, and he could speak out against the corruption and the crooked Nevada gambling intruding into California Indian affairs. He'd come to the Bole Maru five years before when he was an alcoholic and was living a wild lifestyle. When he attended meetings with others of his tribe, he found he could keep the demons at bay with the help of the teachings and his own strength of will.

"I was the stereotypical Native American every white person sees in the movies and on TV," he told anyone who'd listen. "But when I came back to the old ways, I found myself, and now I want to help others of the People return to the true path."

He loved the Bole Maru at once; the combination of traditional Native American beliefs and Victorian-era Christianity intrigued him and drew him in. After he got sober, his grandfather, a tribal medicine man, showed up at his door one day, and over the next few months, Jack learned the history of the Bole Maru.

The movement's origin dated back to 1870, when migrating Pomos first brought word of the Ghost Dance to Northern California from Jack's Great-Great-Grandfather Wovoka, the self-proclaimed messiah of Nevada's Paiute tribe.

Even though Bole Maru stressed cultural purity, the religion ironically borrowed many of its tenets from white culture, including prohibitions against alcohol and gambling.

"When you were born, we named you after your great-great-grandfather, Wovoka. His white man name was Jack Wilson too. When you were three days old, one of our medicine men prophesied you would be a great chief and leader of your people," his grandfather told him.

This lineage made Jack a prime candidate to be the leader of the Bole Maru movement. And if he could find the Ghost Dancer shirt, he would gain great respect among his people. His Native American brothers and sisters put great stock in the ancestors, and to wear Red Bull's shirt would be a sign of strong medicine and of the approval of the ancient ones.

So, Jack had a pressing urgency for his search. Representatives of the Nevada gamblers were sniffing around this ranch, looking for prime sites for a casino. Since old Mrs. Roberts was a direct descendent of Red Bull, the People showed great interest in building a casino here and in turning the ranch into a resort with hotels and Las Vegas-style entertainment. Jack came to the back wall and searched. He found a spot where he could see scuff marks in the dust. The girls' footprints came right to the wall and then stopped. In the flashlight's beam, he saw the tracks disappeared into the wall and then came out again, but he couldn't see a door.

*There must be a way through this wall.* He looked for a handle or a button. The wall had a coat rack with pegs sticking out with ponchos and old dungarees hanging on them. An old monster movie came to his mind where the hero had pulled on a light fixture and the wall opened, so he pulled and pushed on anything looking like a handle. When he grabbed the first peg on the coat rack and heard a click, the panel in front of him slid to the left.

He stooped down and stepped into the passage. The girls' tracks lay in the dirt in front of him. Between the wooden wall and the old stone wall was a space, and to his left, brickwork.

*There's a lot more to this house than meets the eye.*

He stood at the bottom of a shaft. Shining his light upward, he discovered a ladder hanging bolted to the wall, the bottom rung about two feet above his head.

The shaft and the ladder disappeared up into the darkness.

*They must have built this for old Red Bull when he was hiding out here. This took a lot of work!*

He put his flashlight in his pocket and was about to jump up and grab the ladder when he heard a slight sound back in the cellar like a foot turning on a small rock. Pivoting around, he poked his head back through the opening. A board crashed against the back of his head, and he tumbled forward into darkness.

Grandpa Roberts came to his senses slowly. Every bone and muscle in his body ached. He was leaning up against the wall of what looked like a cave. A single candle burned against the darkness. He sensed a dark figure moving toward him, and he tried to lift himself up, but strong hands pushed him back down.

"It's all right. You are safe here."

Grandpa Roberts lifted his good hand and rubbed his head. "Oh boy, what hit me?"

"You need to stay quiet. I will answer your questions in a little while. Now, you need to rest."

The dark figure motioned toward a sleeping bag on a foam pad. Grandpa shifted over to the pad and stretched out. His head hurt like the blazes, and he could feel the cuts and bruises on his face and arms.

"Drink this." The dark figure passed him a cup of a strong-smelling liquid.

Grandpa didn't argue, and he took the cup and drank.

Then the figure laid his hands on Grandpa's arm and spoke in a language he couldn't understand.

Grandpa lay back on the sleeping bag, content to rest for now. The warmth of the liquid stole through his body. One of the last things he remembered seeing before he drifted into sleep was his old flashlight on a shelf in the rock wall next to the bed, with the lens broken out.

Boo stared up at her grandma. "What do you mean, Grandpa's missing?" Grandma looked like she would cry.

"Grandpa went out to check the stock about three hours ago, like he does every day. He always comes back by four o'clock. He's two hours late, and I haven't heard from him. I have a bad feeling. We met with some fellows who wanted us to sell the ranch to the local Indians for a casino. I didn't like their looks. I think they might have done something to Grandpa." As she spoke, Grandma looked at the open door into the clock. "What were you girls doing?"

Boo wasn't sure what to say. "We wanted to tell you Grandma—"

"We found a secret passage behind the clock, Grandma," Punkin interrupted. "It goes all the way to the basement. We think the passage is something Great-Great-Grandpa Jamison built so Red Bull could hide in the house."

Grandma walked to the clock and looked inside. "My word. I've lived here all my life and never knew about any secret passage. I want to see what you found, but right now we've got to go look for Grandpa." She turned and left the room.

Boo pulled Punkin aside and whispered to her. "I noticed you said nothing about the cave."

Punkin grinned. "Well, like you said, there's a mystery here, and who better to solve the case than you and me. Besides, Grandma's so upset, she'd forbid us to go looking in the cave. If Grandpa's missing, I think it'll be up to us to find him."

The old chief looked down at the sleeping form of Grandpa Roberts. As he prayed, Grandpa's face softened, and the pain lines vanished.

The old man spoke to the Lord with a tone of great reverence. "Well, Great Chief, I think his arm will be all right. Thank you for healing him. Now, I better see about helping those girls."

He pulled his hat over his eyes and tightened his cloak around him, and for a moment a flash of brilliant light engulfed him as he stepped out through the door of the cave and vanished.

# CHAPTER NINE
## THE PRISONER

Punkin and Boo followed their grandmother downstairs and out onto the porch. Several ranch hands waited there. Grandma called them all together. "Let's look on all the fire roads. He always goes up the canyon to the north. Red, you and John follow me, and the rest of you fan out to the south and west." She looked over at Punkin and Boo. "Girls, I want you to stay here and keep watch in case your grandpa comes home."

"But Grandma—"

"I don't need you to argue, Boo. Just do as I say. Okay, fellas, let's go." She and the men rushed from the porch toward their vehicles.

The crew climbed into their trucks and ATVs and revved up the motors. Grandma led the way in her Land Rover with Red and John following, and the rest scattered to look for Grandpa.

The two girls watched the rescuers leave and then turned back to the house. Punkin looked worried. "Gosh, Boo, what if those guys hurt Grandpa?"

"I don't know, Punkin, but there's a lot going on here that makes little sense. We have a secret tunnel, some mysterious clues from Great-Great-Grandpa Jamison, local tribes and gamblers trying to buy the ranch, Grandpa's missing, and who knows what else."

"Not to mention the ghost of Red Bull drumming somewhere beneath the house, Boo."

Boo snapped her fingers. "That's it! Whatever's going on has to do with the ghost in the cave, I know it. I think it's time for us to go find out where that passage leads."

Punkin nodded her head. "Okay, but I think you must be braver than me. Look." She held out her arm and showed her cousin the goose bumps all over it.

Boo took Punkin by the arm and steered her toward the house. "Look. We'll be real careful and real quiet. I know there are answers down in that cave, and we need to help Grandpa. So, let's go."

The girls ran up the front steps, grabbed the flashlights from the closet, and headed for the attic.

Jack Wilson woke with a splitting headache.

*Man, what hit me?*

Someone threw cold water in his face. He gasped and tried to lift his arms to defend himself, but someone had tied them behind his back. He was leaning against something hard, and a blindfold covered his eyes.

"Awake at last," a man said in a gruff voice.

"Thanks for showing us the ladder, Jack," another man said. "Or should I call you Wovoka?"

Jack tried to shake the water off. "Who are you guys?"

All he got was a slap to the face.

"Shut up, spirit-boy, or we'll take you out," the second voice said. "We know what you're up to, and I'm telling you that no 'holy Joe' will come along and change our tribe's mind about casinos and—"

"Shut up, you fool," the first man said. He sounded older than the other man. "Just keep your mouth shut."

Jack licked his lip and felt blood running from his mouth.

*So, these guys are tribe members. They must be part of the group that's lined up with those crooks from Las Vegas. I've got to get out of here.*

Someone gripped him by the throat, and the older man spoke to him. "Just tell us what we want to know, and we'll kill you quick and painless."

"What do you want?" Jack choked out.

"We want the Ghost Dance shirt," the younger one answered. "We know that's what you're looking for, but we'll find it first, and when Chief here wears the shirt at the council, he'll get the tribe to go on the warpath by bringing in a casino that'll ruin the area with gambling and everything bad that goes with it—"

The steel grip on Jack's throat was suddenly released. A dull thud that Jack recognized as a fist against a face was followed by the sound of a body hitting the floor.

After a moment's silence, Jack heard someone scrambling to his feet. "Ow, what did you do that for?" the younger man whined.

"I told you to shut up, and I mean it. If you want to end up like Wilson, just keep talking, you idiot."

Jack could hear the younger man muttering. "Okay, okay."

*The old guy must be a tough old buzzard. He knocked the other guy down. The young one called him Chief. I bet that's Billy Running Horse and his nasty little sidekick, Joe Johnson.*

Much more was at stake than Jack had imagined.

Running Horse squeezed Jack's neck again. "Tell us where the shirt is."

Jack tried to figure out a way to fool his captors. "I don't know where it is."

Running Horse punched him in the head.

After a minute, Jack's senses cleared. "Keep doing that, Chief, and you'll kill me before I can tell you."

A cell phone rang. Running Horse answered. "Yeah, what? Yeah, we got Wilson, but he won't tell us where the shirt is. What? Okay, okay."

The phone clicked shut. "Jimmy wants to see us right away."

"What about *him*?"

"What about him, stupid?" Running Horse laughed. "Leave him here. No one will find him. We'll take care of him when we get back."

Their footsteps faded away. It sounded like they were in a cave or a tunnel. He tested the ropes that bound him to the pole. The knots were strong, and he couldn't budge them.

*Great! Looks like I'm in a lot of trouble unless I can get out of here.*

He struggled against the ropes, but whoever tied them knew what they were doing. At last, he dropped his head in frustration, realizing how desperate his situation was. He couldn't get away. Jack gave up struggling and leaned back against the post. Then after a moment, he lifted his head and sang the chant of the Unconquered Spirit.

Boo scooted through the clock. She stepped onto the ladder and turned back to Punkin who had crawled through behind her. "If Red Bull could hang on to the ladder, then we should be able to go together. Come on."

Punkin leaned out, swung onto the ladder, and the girls climbed down together. When she reached the thirteenth rung, Boo felt for the third stone to the left and reached up for the second smooth stone above that one.

"Hold on tight, Punkin." She pushed the hidden lever, and the ladder rotated into the wall and slid down. Both girls held on tightly. The ride ended with a jerk about three feet off the ground. Jumping down, the girls shined their lights down the dark tunnel and then looked at each other.

"Okay, Boo," Punkin gave Boo a wry grin. "If you go, I'll go."

Taking a few steps, the two girls headed down the dark passage. They moved forward, one keeping a light on the floor so they wouldn't trip and the other shining ahead into the darkness. The passage wound downward, and the rocks were black with age and covered with slimy moss. Every few feet, they came to metal holders built into the wall.

Boo pointed them out to Punkin. "This passage must have already been under the hill when Great-Great-Grandpa Jamison built the house in the 1800s. Look how old everything looks. Those holders must have been for torches. Grandpa thinks there was a Spanish mission or a fort here first, and I bet whoever lived here must have found this cave and built that secret entrance into the stone wall."

The girls continued to follow the dark passage down into the hill. They came to a place where the tunnel divided. The left-hand shaft got narrower and sloped downward into the darkness, and the other leveled out and went straight ahead. They hesitated, wondering which way to go.

Boo took hold of Punkin's arm. "Listen. Do you hear that?"

Punkin listened. Down the passage from the right came the sound of a voice. The voice was low-pitched and whoever was there was chanting. She nodded. "It reminds me of the Native American chiefs chanting their songs in the documentary films I watched on the History Channel."

"Shh," Boo cautioned, "it's coming from down there." They tiptoed down the passage until they came to what looked like a dead end. She pointed. "Up there."

Punkin looked up. A faint glimmer of light peeked through a hole above their heads. "Maybe it's the ghost."

Boo didn't wait, but setting down her flashlight, she grabbed hold of some stones sticking out of the wall. She whispered to Punkin, "It's like a climbing wall. I'm going up." She climbed up to the crack where the light was coming through. Peeking through, she saw a figure tied to a post in the middle of a dirt chamber.

She clambered back down. "It's that guy, Jack Wilson, that Grandpa hired a few days ago. He's tied to a post, and he looks like he's bleeding."

"What should we do, Boo?"

"There must be a way into that room, a hidden door that'll get us in there." She picked up her flashlight and shined it around at the base of the wall.

Then Punkin grabbed Boo and pointed off to the right. A big stone set into the wall didn't seem to belong there. Together, the two girls pulled on it, expecting it to be heavy, but to their surprise, the stone popped right out.

Punkin peered into the hole. "We can crawl right through."

Sure enough, the bottom of the wall now had a hole big enough for a grown man to slip through.

Quickly, the girls crawled through and ran to Jack.

Jack turned his head toward the sound when he heard them approach. "Who is it?"

"It's us, Jack, Punkin and Boo. What happened to you?"

"I'll tell you later, girls. First, get this blindfold off and get me loose. Look in my back pocket. There should be a little knife. I don't think they took it."

Punkin pulled the blindfold off while Boo reached into his pocket and pulled out a small folding knife. "I found it, Jack."

"Cut me loose before they come back."

She cut through the rope that bound Jack's feet. While working on the rope holding him to the pole, men's voices sounded outside the room.

Jack whispered, "It's them. They're coming back. Hurry."

Boo cut while Punkin stared at the mouth of the passage leading into the room. The men were coming closer and closer.

Deep in another part of the cave below the ranch, a solitary tree branch adorned with strange amulets and bones stood planted in the ground in the middle of a large room. A strange mist formed, and whispering evil voices spoke.

"He is coming soon. We must bring him to our master."

"Yes," another foul croaking voice said. "We must turn him to the darkness. If he follows us wearing the shirt, the tribes will accept him as leader, and he will see to it that the tribe builds the casino. The evil that follows the gambling will destroy them all. Our master will have many new slaves."

"We must bring him to the dark lord," another voice gurgled.

The voices cackled and howled, and from out of the mist the ghostly sound of a drum filled the room.

# CHAPTER TEN
## A Darker Mystery

Grandma Roberts drove up the fire road above the ranch. This was her favorite place, but today she was so worried about Grandpa she couldn't appreciate the hills sweeping away to the south toward San Francisco Bay, or the dome of Mt. Diablo across the Oakland Hills seventy miles away. She kept her eyes focused on the road, looking for Grandpa's white truck. She was so absorbed that she missed the signs at the side of the road.

From behind her on an ATV, Red came roaring up alongside her truck and yelled at her. "There's skid marks back there, Rose! We better go look." He swerved around and thundered back down the road.

Grandma's heart leapt up into her throat. She stopped the truck, jumped out, and ran back to where Red crouched at the top of the bank, pointing down the hill. "There! It's the truck, Rose."

About one hundred feet below them, Grandpa's white truck lay jammed against a tree upside down.

"Oh, dear Lord!" Grandma cried out as she placed her hand over her heart. "We've got to get down there."

Red grabbed Grandma and held her. "Go easy, Rose. John and I will find him."

The two ranch hands scrambled down the steep bank, pushing their way through the Manzanita and Sage scrub. When they got to the truck, they looked inside.

John yelled up to Grandma. "He's not in here, Rose."

"Look around the truck and see if he got thrown out."

Red and John conducted a thorough search of the area. After about ten minutes, Red yelled back up. "Rose, he's nowhere around here, and I don't know where he could be. He's not under the truck, and the sides of the gully would've forced him to roll out somewhere near here if he got thrown out. It flattens out here, so he wouldn't have slid any further."

"Look once more, please."

Red and John searched again. Finally, Red shouted up to Grandma. "He's not here, Rose! There's not a trace of him."

Grandma put her face in her hands. "Oh, James, James, where are you?"

Billy Running Horse and Weasel Joe didn't like what Las Vegas Jimmy had to say to them. They had driven to a motel in Ukiah and met Jimmy and his two thugs. Jimmy's henchman didn't sit during the meeting but stood with arms crossed, the bulges of the guns under their coats obvious to the two nervous men.

"Billy, I've given you a month to take care of this business, but now I'm getting pressure from my connections in Las Vegas. They want a casino in southern Sonoma County, and they want it now. They have twenty million dollars to buy land, and all they need is your tribe to front the deal. You get the Robertses to sell, and we turn around and sell it to my friends and split the rest."

Running Horse shook his head. "Sorry, Jimmy. We tried hard, but Roberts and his wife won't sell, and that's the most obvious place for a reservation and casino. The old lady is one-quarter Lakota Sioux, and that means Ghost Dancer Ranch has been in Native American hands since John Jamison married Red Bull's daughter. It's a natural—there's no other piece of property around Petaluma big enough to do what you want to do. So, the next step is getting Roberts out of the way. Is he dead yet?"

Jimmy stood. He pushed himself right into Running Horse's face and made his point in a low but brutal tone. "Don't question me about my end of the deal. I've already given you and your low-life friend here twenty grand to get this deal done. If you want the rest of the finder's fee, just do your job. Don't worry about Roberts. I'll take him care of today. By tonight, he'll be dead. It should be easy then to convince old Rosie that without Grandpa, she can't run the ranch. Wave some more green in front of her face. Offer her ten million, and she'll give in. But first, make the Wilson kid disappear. I want your tribe behind this casino when we put it all together, and there better not be any competition for tribal leadership. I don't want Jack Wilson telling the tribe that casinos are bad. Now, get out of here and do what I told you, or you can forget about this deal."

The two men beat a hasty retreat out the door while Jimmy turned around to deal with his henchmen. "I'm giving you two morons one more chance to take care of Roberts, and this time there's no room for mistakes."

"But, Boss, I don't know what happened to the old guy." The big henchman, Pete, shrugged. "We hit him square on with the boulder and knocked his truck off the cliff. He should be dead. I swear somebody helped him, because he disappeared. He couldn't have walked away. There were no tracks. Am I right, Artie?"

"That's what happened, Boss."

Jimmy didn't have a happy look on his face. "Shut up! I don't want your lame excuses. Just find that old man and finish him. Now, get out of here before I find replacements for you two stooges."

After they left, Jimmy sat alone in the room. "I better pull this off, because my neck is on the line. If I don't make my bones on this one, there won't be a next one."

# THE MYSTERY OF GHOST DANCER RANCH

Billy Running Horse and Weasel drove back to the outskirts of the ranch. They hid their truck in the brush and made their way to an old tunnel hidden behind a grove of redwood trees on the east side of the hill leading up to the house.

"We were lucky to find this place, so close to the ranch and all." Weasel pushed aside the scrub hiding the entrance.

Billy shoved the younger man inside. "You won't be so lucky if you don't find that shirt. There's more to this tunnel than we know. I'm sure old Red Bull's Ghost Dancer shirt is somewhere in the tunnels under the house, and we need to get whatever information Wilson's uncovered while he's been snooping around. I think this tunnel somehow connects to the ladder Wilson found in the cellar. We've got to get back in there and see where that leads."

The pair of crooks went into the tunnel, picked up the flashlights they left at the entrance, then hurried back toward the room where they held Jack Wilson prisoner.

"We'll be rich if we pull this off." Weasel punched Billy on the arm. "Not only do we get the finder's fee from Las Vegas Jimmy, but we'll be in charge of the council that runs the casino. Lots of chances to do a little skimming, eh Billy?"

"You are such an idiot." Running Horse shook his head and kept walking. "Nothing is for sure until we have that shirt in our hands—and the deed to the ranch, so just do your job and shut your pie-hole."

"One of these days I'll shut *you* up if you don't quit calling me an idiot," Weasel muttered under his breath.

The two men made their way deeper into the tunnel under the hill. When they came to a fork in the tunnel, they turned left. As they came around a corner, they saw a stout wooden door set into the rock wall of the cave with a strong padlock on the bolt.

Weasel pulled a key out of his pocket and unlocked the door. "This old storage room makes a great jail, don't it?"

As they stepped inside, both stopped with their mouths open. The ropes lay at the foot of the post along with the blindfold. Jack Wilson had vanished!

Punkin, Boo, and Jack Wilson hurried down the tunnel. They'd cut Jack loose moments before the men returned, and the three of them had squeezed through the opening into the passage behind the storage room. Wilson had pushed the rock back into place a moment before Running Horse and Weasel walked into the room.

"We've got to get Jack back to the ladder." Boo helped Jack as he limped along. Behind them, they heard the shouts of the two men as they discovered their prisoner was missing.

Jack was having a hard time walking. "It won't take long for them to find that rock, girls. There's no other way out of that room except the door. We've got to hurry."

As they came to the junction with the older narrower tunnel, Punkin felt something like a hand on her shoulder, pushing her toward the dark opening. She stopped, puzzled.

"Did you push me, Boo?"

"No, why?"

She pointed to the narrow entrance that led into the side tunnel. "I have the strangest feeling we should go down this way."

Someone groaned behind them. They turned and saw Jack slumped against the wall. He looked terrible, and the wound on his face was bleeding again.

"I can't climb up any ladders today, girls."

Punkin grabbed Jack's arm. "Come on, Boo, let's get him down this tunnel and find a hiding place." The two of them helped him slowly make his way along the wall and finally got him into the narrow tunnel. They made their way downward. At last, they came to what appeared to be a dead end. Boo shined her light around but could only see a blank wall.

"Now what?" she asked.

Something puzzled Punkin. She was sure they were supposed to go this way. "I don't know. It looks like we have to go back."

Then Boo pointed to a rock set in the wall above their heads, smoother than the surrounding rocks and barely visible in the light. "Wait a minute, Punkin. Look up there."

Punkin nodded. "It's just like the smooth rocks that make the ladder work." She reached up and pressed on the rock. With a quiet click, the end of the tunnel opened like a door. Behind them were the tunnel and the two angry crooks. Ahead was a set of steps carved into the floor of the cave that led down into darkness.

Jack glanced back. The sounds of pursuit were coming closer. "We can't go back. They'll find us for sure."

Gathering their courage, Punkin and Boo helped Jack down the stairs into the deep darkness of the cave.

A dark figure watched from the shadows as the three made their way down the stairs. "These are brave girls, worthy to be warriors, and I will help them as I can, Lord. If they can face the darkness, perhaps they will discover the secret of the cave. Then they can solve the mystery and drive the evil away." The figure slipped down the stairs behind them.

# CHAPTER ELEVEN
## A Fearful Place

When Grandpa Roberts woke, he was alone. He ached in every part of his body, but he felt much stronger than he had when he passed out.

*Something in that drink …*

He looked around the room, but nobody was with him. "I better get out of here. Rose doesn't know where I am, and she may have found the truck by now." He pulled himself up to a sitting position and sat on the edge of the rough bunk he was lying on. He felt his arm. "Funny, I could have sworn I broke this arm." He saw he was in a cave or a tunnel of some sort. "I knew these canyons were full of caves, and I've found some of them, but I don't recognize this one."

The candle gave a low light from the shelf on the wall. Grandpa saw his old yellow flashlight next to it. "How in the world did that get here?"

He remembered the wreck and the voices of the men coming to get him. He'd bet they had something to do with that crook, Billy Running Horse. *He was none too happy when Rosie and I turned him down.* Those poor folks thought the answer to all their problems laid in building casinos. But the tribes didn't make that much. The members made a few dollars, but most of the money went into the hands of the Las Vegas gangsters who financed the casino. And then the local people would get hooked on the gambling, and the next thing anyone knew, folks would be stealing and committing other crimes to support their gambling. *Not to mention how it would change the spiritual values of the whole community with the alcohol and drugs that would come in. And the shows they put on in the clubs are merely more of that sewage they call entertainment these days.*

*No, a casino is not going on my land. Even though Rosie inherited it from her dad, I have been here for almost fifty years, and no snake from Las Vegas will get his hands on it.*

Grandpa Roberts eased himself up and waited for a minute until the dizziness passed, then he stepped over to the shelf and picked up the flashlight. He clicked it on, and a strong steady beam shot out. "I've had this flashlight since I was a Boy Scout, and it's never failed me yet. Sure is a good thing it's here."

He pointed the light around the cave until he discovered what looked like the way out. He took a few tentative steps and came to a low passage that turned right and went away into the darkness. Supporting himself with one hand on the wall, Grandpa moved off and carefully stepped down the tunnel.

Soon, he saw a dim light ahead. As he walked toward it, he realized it came through a narrow opening in the rock. A thick screen of manzanita scrub and Scotch broom blocked the entrance, but when he pushed through it, he knew right where he was.

"Why, I've walked past this place a hundred times and never thought to look for a cave here." The sun had already set over the western ridge, and the woods were growing dark.

Grandpa headed back to where he crashed the truck. As he approached the spot, he heard voices and saw the gleam of flashlights among the trees. "Keep looking, Red, he's got to be here somewhere!" He recognized Rose's voice.

"Hey, I'm here!" He cried out to the searchers. "Rose, over here!"

"James, James!" Grandma answered him from up on the road. "Oh, thank God! Where have you been?"

Red and John came running through the brush and stopped short when they saw him.

Red scratched his head. "James? Are you okay?"

Both of them stared at Grandpa with looks of amazement on their faces.

Grandpa chuckled. "Yeah, boys, I'm fine. A little stiff and sore, but other than that, I think I'll live."

"Where were you?" John stepped closer and looked around.

Grandpa gingerly moved his arm up and down a few times. "It's the darndest thing. I know I broke this arm when I rolled the truck. Then somebody carried me back to a cave over that way and gave me some stuff that made me feel better, and now my arm works fine. I have a few cuts and bruises, but I think I'm okay."

Grandma scrambled down the bank and threw her arms around Grandpa. "Oh, James, dear, I thought you were dead." Then she put her face on Grandpa's chest and cried.

"There, there, Rosie." Grandpa patted her shoulder. "I'm fine. I'm just fine."

"Well," said a quiet voice behind them. "That may not last too long, Grandpa."

The four of them turned around to stare down the barrels of some nasty looking guns, held by two even nastier looking thugs.

Punkin and Boo helped Jack down the stairs. As they did, they heard the door click shut behind them. The stairs spiraled down into pitch darkness. Even their flashlights didn't give much light.

A shiver ran down Punkin's back. "I don't like this place. It feels, dark and … and …"

"And evil," Jack said. The girls drew closer to the young man and clung to his arms. The darkness pressed in on them like it had substance and they could barely force themselves to keep going.

Boo stopped. "I will not fear any darkness." A Bible Scripture popped into her mind. Something her youth pastor had taught.

She whispered into the darkness. "Greater is he that is in me, than he that is in the world …" She cleared her throat and said it again, louder this time. "Greater is he that is in me, than he that is in the world!"

Either her eyes were getting used to the dark, or the words Boo said had power, for as she stood there, the thick darkness drew back, and she could see around them.

They continued down the stairs and stepped into a large room. A bitter smell lingered in the air. In the center of the room was a rough pile of rocks with a dead tree branch stuck on top of it, decorated with what looked like religious offerings.

Jack looked at the pile of rocks and the tree branch. "This is a place where they do the Ghost Dance. This is an altar. The dancers form a circle around it and dance for hours day and night, on and on, chanting while they dance. The whole idea is to get in contact with the spirits of their ancestors. After they dance for a long time, they go into a trance and fall to the ground. The men who pass out are 'dead' and while they are unconscious, they have visions of their ancestors. The visions always end with a chant describing a great encampment of all the Native Americans who have ever died where there is no sorrow but only joy."

Boo drew closer to Jack. "The Bible says it's not right to call up the spirits of the dead, Jack. King Saul called up the spirit of Samuel, and he died in battle the next day. This place doesn't feel right. It's dark and just wrong. Did you notice how the darkness seemed to draw back when I quoted the Bible? That shows me that there's something evil here, and I don't want to find it."

Even as Boo spoke there came the sound of a drum. The single beat reverberated off the walls, even though seemingly from a long way off.

"It's Red Bull's ghost." Punkin grabbed Boo and held on. Jack took hold of the girls and stepped back.

Boo could feel a shudder run through Jack's body.

And as the drum beat louder and louder, the malignant darkness closed in on them.

Boo had never felt such deep, suffocating tentacles of fear before.

Punkin, Boo, and Jack couldn't see him, but the old bronzed man stood behind them in the dark. As he felt their fear overtake them, he prayed, "Lord, help them remember that they can do all things through you, who strengthens them. Help them know whence comes their help. Lift the hands that hang down and strengthen the feeble knees. They war not against flesh and blood, but against principalities and powers and spiritual beings in high places."

As he prayed, he sensed the Holy Spirit fill the room, and he knew the Lord had heard his prayer.

# CHAPTER TWELVE
## A Cry For Help!

Weasel Joe stared in disbelief at the cut ropes and the empty post.

Running Horse pointed at the walls. "We locked the door when we left, so there's got to be another way out of this room. Look for it—now!"

The two men searched around the walls of the room.

Weasel bent over and walked along the wall, studying the ground. Then he stood and motioned to Running Horse. "Hey, over here, Billy. Look at this." He pointed to tracks and scuff marks in the dust that looked like they emerged right out of the wall and then went back into it. "Someone came through here—two people it looks like—and then the three of them went back.

Running Horse got down on his knees and looked at the wall. "There's a big rock here that's not like the rest of the wall. Let's push on it."

The men pushed and the rock moved a little.

"It's moving, Billy, push harder."

They pushed again, and the big rock popped out the other side, exposing an opening in the wall.

Billy grabbed a flashlight and stuck his head through the opening. "There's another tunnel here all right. Come on, let's find that rat."

The two men squeezed through the small opening into the passage behind the storage room. The tunnel led off to the right, so they took off at a run to find Wilson and whoever had helped him. When they got to the end, all they saw was a blank wall—a dead end.

Weasel shined his light on the face of the rock wall. "Man, there must be more to this wall than we're seeing. Look for another rock, like the one back there."

They hunted around the base of the wall until they saw another rock that looked like the one blocking the opening in the storeroom.

Running horse dropped to his knees. "Push on it, quick."

Weasel got down, and they pushed. The rock moved, but this time it had a different result. Instead of opening into another tunnel, the floor beneath them swung open, and they fell screaming into a deep darkness. Their screaming stopped when they slammed into the floor ten feet below and passed out.

Grandpa and Grandma Roberts, Red, and John lay hogtied in the back of the crooks' pickup.

Las Vegas Jimmy's two henchmen sat in the front seat of the truck.

Artie glanced back through the window at the prisoners. "Should we take them to Jimmy or just get rid of them?"

Pete grimaced. "I'm not sure, Artie. I think we messed this up. We were just supposed to take care of Roberts, so it would scare the old lady into selling the ranch. Now we have to figure out what to do with four people instead of one."

"I say we knock them all out, Pete, and roll the other truck down the hill too. Then it'll look like they all got killed in the wreck."

"No." Pete shook his head. "First, we have to find out who inherits the ranch when the Roberts are dead. I bet it's one of those girls staying at the ranch."

"So, what do we do with them until then, Pete?"

Pete started the truck. "Let's take them to that old line shack way back in the hills we found when we were scouting this place out. We'll tie them up good and call Jimmy."

"Right, Pete. Jimmy will know what to do. Let's go."

Pete put the truck in gear and drove off up the road heading for the shack. He came to a fork in the road and pulled over, trying to remember the way. Suddenly, a strange creaking sound echoed outside. He glanced out the window and to his horror, saw a giant tree tearing loose from the bank and falling straight toward them.

"Look out, Artie!" Pete yelled as the tree crashed down on the cab of the truck. He did his best to become very small as Artie screamed and rolled onto the floor. With a screech of tearing metal, the roof crushed down on them.

Punkin, Boo, and Jack stood transfixed in the middle of the room. The girls had scooted as close to Jack as they could get. The throbbing drum grew louder and louder, like it was coming from all around them.

Punkin shook like a leaf. "What is it, Jack?"

Jack pulled the girls close. "It's a Ghost Dance drummer, Punkin. Someone has used this place for the Ghost Dance, but not for a long, long time."

As they huddled together, Jack saw strange, formless shapes, like faces in the darkness. The faces became clearer until he realized they were standing in the middle of a circle of luminous green figures. The figures were going around them in a circle, shuffling in an awkward sliding sidestep.

Jack stared in amazement. "These are like the spirits of my ancestors, doing the Ghost Dance, but I don't understand. I was always told that the Ghost Dance was big medicine, and that it was a holy and sacred ritual. This is not holy. It's evil."

The circle of ghastly dancers closed in around them. A horrible voice spoke to Jack. "Join us, Jack Wilson, and we will give you all the kingdoms of this world, your people will follow you to freedom from the whites, and you will be great in the sight of all men."

A sudden strength rose in Jack's spirit. "No, No, you are evil! I shall not follow you!" Then he remembered something.

"Boo!" he cried out. "Remember what happened when you quoted the Bible?"

"I don't think just Scripture alone will scare these guys!" Boo yelled back. "We need to use something else. Evil spirits and demons are real. My pastor saw lots of people possessed by demons in Africa. They're not just stories."

"What did your pastor do?"

"He told me we may use the name of Jesus against any enemy, real or spirit," she said. "So, he commanded them to come out in the name of Jesus. It always worked."

"Go for it, Boo!" Punkin shouted.

Boo stepped in front of the other two and shouted at the top of her lungs, "In the name of Jesus, help us Lord, and drive these evil things away!"

A brilliant light flashed in front of them, followed by the screams of the demons as they rushed off into the darkness.

As they did, Punkin, Boo, and Jack fell on the floor unconscious.

As Punkin, Boo, and Jack lay there, the bright figure, no longer looking like an old Native American but now tall and bronze with a great flaming sword in his hand, stood guard over them and drove back the darkness.

# CHAPTER THIRTEEN
## UNDER THE CROSS

Running Horse woke up in pitch darkness.

Beside him Weasel groaned. "Man, where are we?"

"I don't know, Joe, but I think I broke my arm."

Weasel grabbed him. "Hey, do you see that weird light?"

Running Horse stared into the darkness. The room seemed to be getting lighter. Then horrible luminous green faces took shape in the air above them. This time he grabbed Weasel. "What's that ... What is that?" He could feel Weasel shaking.

"I, I don't know, Billy, faces, weird faces ..."

Then the sound of a drum filled the chamber and the light grew brighter, as hideous figures slowly closed in on Billy and Weasel. The drum grew louder and louder, but it couldn't drown out the screams of the two terrified men.

When the tree hit the truck, it bounced Red right out the back. The ropes binding him broke as though they were string when he hit the ground.

"Woof," Red grunted as the hard road knocked the wind out of him. Then he realized he was free. He pulled off the ropes and stood. Muffled cries sounded from the flattened cab of the truck.

"Help, help, we're being crushed!" Artie cried out from inside the cab.

"We're trapped under the tree!" Pete yelled out. "Get us out of here, quick!"

Red ran up to the cab and checked out the two crooks. When he saw they were just pinned and in no danger of being crushed, he grinned. "Well, boys, I think I'll just let you sit a spell under that lovely tree, while I help my boss and the missus out of these ropes. And then I think we'll call the sheriff and have him send a 'jaws of life' up here to get you boys out. But where you're headed will be just as tight, I reckon." And smiling to himself, Red set about freeing Grandma and Grandpa and his friend John.

Punkin, Boo, and Jack woke up in the dark, but the evil that had tried to attack them before was gone.

Boo felt around on the floor until she found her flashlight. When she switched on the light, she saw Jack sitting with his head in his hands.

He looked up at her and she could see tears running down his face.

Punkin put her hand on his shoulder. "Why are you crying, Jack?"

He looked at the girls and wiped his eyes with the back of his sleeve. With the bruises and cuts on his face where Running Horse had hit him, and the tear streaks through the dust on his face, he looked quite the sight. "I'm not sure. I think … well, let me begin at the beginning." He took a deep breath.

"I used to be a drunk, But I got some help. After I got sober, my grandfather came to visit me. He told me he'd been waiting for me to straighten out my life, because he knew it was my destiny to bring peace to my people and restore us to our lands. He told me

I could do it if I revived the Ghost Dance. He told me about my ancestor, Wovoka, who walked the Ghost Dance trail in peace.

"He told me that in Wavoka's time, many of the chiefs could not bear to live in peace with the white man and they twisted Wovoka's message. They told their tribes the Ghost Dance was the trail of war, that the only way to drive the whites out was by the gun and the tomahawk, and with the great medicine of the Ghost Dance, they would become invulnerable to harm in battle.

"Red Bull was one of these chiefs. He was with Kicking Bear when they visited Wovoka in Nevada. Wovoka explained to them that Native Americans had to live right and shun the ways of the whites—and walk in peace with the white man. Wovoka asked that instead of war, the people would pray, meditate, and dance the Ghost Dance in peace.

"But Kicking Bear would not listen. He returned to the Dakotas with Red Bull and stirred up Sitting Bull to make the warpath. Sitting Bull defeated Custer at the battle of the Little Big Horn, and the soldiers wanted revenge. So, they found Sitting Bull and killed him and then went on a rampage at Wounded Knee. They massacred many women and children.

"Red Bull fled for his life. When he came to this ranch, he had a Ghost Dancer shirt that Wovoka gave him, but when the army captured Red Bull at Ukiah, he didn't have the shirt. My grandfather told me that if I could find the shirt, I would become the chief of all the tribes seeking the renewal and restoration of the Native American race, but only if I walked the trail of peace. So, the reason I came here was to find it."

While Jack quietly told his story, Punkin noticed something. "Look, Boo," she whispered. "The mark of his boot heel is the same one we saw in the cellar."

Jack nodded. "Yes, I was down there before you girls were. I've been hiding out around the ranch for many days looking for the shirt. I finally got your grandpa to hire me so it would be easier to poke around. I always thought the Ghost Dance was good. When we saw those evil spirits mimicking the Ghost Dance, I knew somehow I was wrong, so now I don't know what to do. I love the traditions and ceremonies of my people, but something happened here that twisted everything Wovoka was trying to do. And those men, Running Horse and Weasel, were trying to find the shirt to lead my people in the way of evil. I want to help my people, but I cannot see the way. And that's why I weep."

Punkin sat down beside him. "That's an incredible story, Jack. You know, I have a sense that there is a better ending to the story of Red Bull than we know."

Jack shook his head. "I don't know what it would be. It's obvious that someone did the Ghost Dancing in this room, and I'm guessing Red Bull was the leader. Maybe there's something here that will tell us the rest of the story."

They stood and shined the flashlight around the room. They soon realized the room was a large circle, but the walls were made of adobe bricks, not stone.

Boo got excited. "I bet the Spanish had something here, before Grandpa Jamison built the old ranch house, like a fort—"

"Or a church," Punkin said. The three of them worked their way around the room.

"Look, Jack!" Boo pointed to something on the wall of the cave. "There's a drawing here."

Jack examined the drawing. "It's a pictograph, a Native American symbol. They always mean something." He looked closer. "It's a bull, it's red, and it's walking."

"There are birds above its head," Punkin said, pointing to another part of the drawing.

Jack counted the small dark birds circling the red bull. "There are fifteen."

"What does that mean, Jack?" Boo asked.

"Well, the bull is walking, so maybe it means take fifteen steps in the direction the bull is facing." They counted fifteen steps along the wall.

When they stopped, Punkin pointed to the wall. "Look, there's a small cross here on the wall."

"With a point on the bottom," Boo said.

Jack smiled at the girls. "Let's dig right here. This is a message from Red Bull."

They dug at the foot of the wall. Jack used his small knife and soon they reached boards set into the floor. As they pulled them out and cleared away the dirt, they discovered a natural passage that ran down under the wall, big enough for them to crawl through.

"We must go in." Punkin looked at Jack. "Somehow I know the answer is in there."

Jack crawled in first, and the girls came right after. They slid down the passage into another room, smaller and more cave-like, below the main chamber. In the middle of the back wall was a niche. Placed in the niche was a beautiful silver cross. Under the cross was a carved wooden box. The three of them walked over to the niche and stared at the box. The intricate design on the dark red wood gleamed in the flashlight's beam.

Boo picked up the box and tried to open it, but it was locked.

Punkin looked at the lock and then she remembered something. "The key in Grandma's desk, Boo. Remember how it was so odd shaped? I think it might fit this box."

"Girls," Jack said. "I think we may have just solved the mystery of Ghost Dancer Ranch."

High on the ridge behind the ranch, a dark figure stood looking down on the valley. The figure spoke. "I will lift mine eyes unto the hills. Whence cometh my help? My help cometh from the Lord, which made heaven and earth."

Then the old man smiled as he turned and disappeared over the brow of the hill.

# CHAPTER FOURTEEN
## THE CARVED BOX

Everyone gathered together around the table in the big fireplace room of the old farmhouse. Grandma and Grandpa Roberts, Punkin and Boo, Jack Wilson, Red and John were all there. The carved box sat on the table.

Grandma Roberts held the key with the large circle of metal fastened to the shaft. She untied the piece of white cotton muslin cloth embellished with the figure of an eagle on it and spread it out beside the box.

"Go ahead, Grandma." Boo nudged her. "We're dying to see what's in the box."

Grandma inserted the key into the lock on the box. It fit!

"I knew it!" Punkin grabbed Boo.

Grandma turned the key, and the lock clicked. She opened the lid, and they all crowded around to look. The box contained several items. The first was a large, red, leather-covered Bible. Grandma lifted the Book out, opened it and read the inscription.

"This is my Bible, given me by my friend, John Jamison, October 19, 1894, and its truth has set me free." Grandma put her hand to her heart. "And it's signed by Red Bull."

Boo opened her eyes wide. "Wow, Grandma, Red Bull was a Christian too."

Jack Wilson stared at the Bible with a strange look on his face.

Grandma placed the Bible down on the table and lifted out the next item, a piece of rolled-up parchment tied with a leather thong. Grandma unrolled and spread it out. They had to put the Bible on one end and a paperweight on the other to keep it flat.

Grandma pulled a pair of reading glasses out of her pocket and examined the paper. "It's in Spanish, I think. I can't read it."

John stepped forward. "I can read Spanish."

He bent down and scanned the document. "It looks like an official document with a seal at the bottom." He looked up at the people around the table. "It's signed by General Vallejo. It's hard for me to read, but from what I can make out, this is the original Spanish Land Grant given to John Jamison. The date is 1881."

Grandpa chimed in from the chair. "What does it say?"

John looked back and mumbled in Spanish as he read and then looked up again. "Well, there's a lot of technical stuff but here's what it says." He read in English.

I, General Mariano Guadalupe Vallejo, Special Commissioner of the Supreme Government of the Country of Mexico and California for the distribution and possession of vacant lands in this Colony, declare that John Jamison has been received as a colonist in the above Colonization Enterprise, and that said John Jamison, having proved that he is of good character and a true friend to the citizens of Rancho Petaluma, shall receive from the country of Mexico, real, actual, virtual and corporal possession of the land known as Rancho San Francisco that occupies the site and grounds of the former Catholic Mission de San Francisco.

Punkin clapped her hands. "I knew it. It was an old Spanish church."

Grandma looked at the parchment. "What else, John?"

John shrugged. "It says the land is your family's land forever. And signed by the General himself."

"Wow! A Spanish Land Grant." Boo touched the parchment gently.

Grandma rolled up the paper and tied it again. Then laying the grant to one side, she reached into the box and took out what looked like a journal bound with engraved leather. She opened the cover and stopped at the flyleaf.

"This is Red Bull's journal. My grandfather," she said.

Jack Wilson stepped closer. "Read it, please."

Everyone turned in surprise, for Jack had been silent until now.

"I must know the truth if I am ever to help my people."

The phone rang, and Grandpa went to answer it. They could hear talking, and then they heard Grandpa say, "What?" There were a few more words and then Grandpa hung up and came back into the room.

"That was the sheriff. He found those two fellas, Running Horse and the guy they call Weasel, down in the cave. They were in a pit at the end of a tunnel. The Sheriff had to climb down to get them, and when they brought them out, they were carrying on and mumbling about 'spirits of the old ones.' The amazing thing was that the sheriff said their hair had turned white. Now doesn't that beat all?"

Boo looked at Jack and Punkin. She knew exactly what Running Horse and Weasel had seen.

Grandma pointed to the chairs around the table. "Sit down all of you. There's a lot here to read."

So, they all sat down, and Grandma read aloud to the group.

Las Vegas Jimmy awoke with a start. He had dozed off in the chair waiting for his boys to call. Someone was knocking at the motel room door. He opened it.

"Hi ya, Jimmy, what's up with you?" the tall, dark man standing in the doorway hissed. Behind him two more men in long dark coats and sunglasses stood, the bulges under their coats visible in the growing dusk.

"Vinnie, what are you doing here?" Jimmy croaked.

"The boys in Vegas sent us to see about our investment." He pushed his way into the room and took Jimmy by the throat. "We heard it ain't going so good over here, so Sal sent me to pick you up. We're going for a little ride."

The two goons each took an arm, and Jimmy slumped between them.

"Can't I gather up my things first?" he whispered.

Vinnie leaned in close and whispered, "Jimmy, I don't think you'll need them."

# CHAPTER FIFTEEN
## RED BULL'S JOURNAL

This is my account in my own writing. I am the war chief, Red Bull, and this is my story of how I found the true path. The year was 1891, and mine was the path of war.

Punkin and Boo leaned forward on their chairs while Jack Wilson put his head down and leaned on his knees. Grandma read on.

After the massacre at Wounded Knee, I took my wife, Chumani, and my daughter, Hantaywee, and fled the soldiers. We came after many trials to California and the Petaluma Adobe of General Mariano Vallejo, seeking refuge from the American government, who wished to hang me. When we came to Petaluma, we found that General Vallejo had died. Not knowing what to do, we felt hopeless. One of Vallejo's trusted men told us of a white man who lived on a ranch given him by Vallejo and was a friend to all people. He sent us to meet this man. And that was how we came to know the white man, Jamison. When he heard of our trouble, he was kind to us and offered us shelter at his home.

Grandma stopped for a moment and pulled a hanky from her pocket.

Boo pulled on her sweater. "Go on, Grandma."

Grandma wiped a tear from her eye. "Wait just a minute, my dear. This is very emotional for me." She collected herself and then went on.

At first, I did not know why the rancher, Jamison, treated us well. He gave us a room in the attic of his house, and together we built an escape passage in the crawl space between the back wall of the house and the stone wall behind it. First, we built the secret door behind the clock, and then I worked on a ladder down to the basement. While I was working on the ladder, I discovered the secret passage the Spanish monks had built into the stones when it was part of their mission.

## July 1891

Though early morning, the day was already turning hot at the ranch. Jamison left for several days to take care of some cattle, and Red Bull was in the escape passage, building the ladder to the basement. He still didn't understand why the rancher had taken him in.

Red Bull's experience with white men had only been with the soldiers who guarded the reservations. They were a sorry lot, sent to the frontier to get them out of the hair of more civilized commands, and most of them hated his people with a passion. Red Bull hated them in return because they were robbing the villages of the food and cattle sent by the Great White Father in Washington, keeping it for themselves and leaving the reservation on starvation rations.

Then Kicking Bear told him of Wovoka, and his new Ghost Dance religion. They traveled to Nevada to see for themselves. The religion captured Red Bull's imagination, and he became a committed dancer. Wovoka recognized something special in Red Bull and gave him a beautiful shirt to wear while dancing.

All the Ghost Dancers wished to have the trance experience where they saw their ancestors in the coming "heaven on earth" reserved only for the People. Red Bull had experiences while dancing, but he was looking for something deeper that would give him power.

Then came the white men who murdered Sitting Bull, and who instigated the massacre at Wounded Knee, and were afraid the Ghost Dancers were building up to a rebellion. Many of the warriors, Red Bull included, wanted only to take the warpath again and drive the white men from their lands or die trying.

In the terrible days after the massacre, Red Bull fled to Petaluma, taking the Ghost Dancer shirt, and now a white man who had shown him nothing but kindness was hiding him. Jamison's care for his family puzzled Red Bull, but the chief intended to take full advantage of Jamison's foolishness.

Red Bull climbed down a rope from the attic, looking for the best way to attach the ladder to the wall in the secret passage. Jamison had given him a miner's cap with a carbide lamp on it, and by its light he noticed a descending line of holes in the rock face, as though someone had already hung a ladder there once. The holes went down the wall, and it was clear someone meant for them to hold metal brackets.

He lowered himself further, and as he reached about fifteen feet above the floor, his moccasin slipped off the stones, and he swung against the wall. As he twisted on the rope, he saw that the impact of his body had caused a section of the wall to swing in, revealing a dark opening.

Red Bull checked around on the wall and found the trigger he'd bumped against—a smooth stone set among rougher larger stones. He pressed it, and the wall swung shut. Curious, he opened the secret door again and swung into the opening.

He stood on the edge of the doorway. A dark shaft went down into the dark below him. Then he saw the ends of some rusty chains dangling against the now open section of the wall. They had come out of two small circular holes in the top of the swinging door when it opened. Brackets were attached to the ends of the chains. He pulled on the chains, and they came through the holes and then stopped. Red Bull could see that if someone attached a section of the ladder to the chains, it would slide down into the hidden shaft when the secret door opened. He looked down into the shaft and saw a huge boulder below him, so he took hold of the rope and lowered himself hand over hand onto the boulder. Then he inched forward until he came to the edge and looked down into the mouth of a passage below him.

Looking up, he could see how the door and ladder worked. As the door swung open and the chains came out of the holes, the section of the ladder attached to the chains would slide down the wall and lower whoever was on it to this stone. Then they could climb down into the passage.

As he gazed around, he discovered another small, smooth stone in the wall like the trigger stone he had bumped to open the door. He pushed it, and the swinging section of the wall above him closed. He pushed it again, and the wall opened.

Red Bull shinnied up the rope and climbed back into the attic. He went to the ranch blacksmith shop and gathered up iron bolts and brackets Jamison had made. Then he went back to the attic and worked his way down the wall, fastening the bolts and brackets into the holes as he went.

He worked through the day, and by nightfall he had constructed a ladder in three parts. He anchored two sections to the wall and hung one on the chains.

Once he finished everything, he stopped for the day and joined his wife and daughter for a meal and rest

In the morning, Red Bull returned to the passage with torches in a bag he slipped over his shoulder. He climbed down the ladder to the section hanging on the secret door, gripped the ladder with one hand, and with the other, he pressed the smooth stone. The secret door swung open, and the ladder slid down the wall into the darkness until it reached the end of the chains.

By the light of his carbide lamp, he could see the ground was just below him, and he jumped down onto the rock. Red Bull looked around, and in a few moments, he discovered footholds cut into the face of the boulder. He climbed down and came to the head of a tunnel leading down into the hill under the house, pulled a torch out of the bag, and lit it.

The tunnel appeared to be a large natural cave. Rough walls dripped with moisture as he made his way downward into the heart of the hill. Along the tunnel, massive beams shored up the ceiling. After a while, he came to a fork in the tunnel. He entered the left-hand opening.

This tunnel was narrower, darker, and descended further down until it came to a dead end. Red Bull held the torch up and searched the blank wall for any kind of lever or door. Another smooth stone set in the tunnel's wall caught his eye, and when he pushed on it, the end of the tunnel swung open, revealing carved steps leading further into the darkness. He climbed down the steps until he came into a large, circular room dug into the heart of the hill. Perfect. He could dance the Ghost Dance there with no interference from Jamison.

It occurred to him there might be another entrance from outside. He returned to the fork in the tunnel and followed the other branch to another dead end. Puzzled, he examined the wall, and a few minutes later, he found a large smooth stone set in the wall's base. He pushed on it, then pulled, and it popped out. Holding the torch ahead, Red Bull crawled through the hole and into a large room. Chains with iron rings hung from the walls, with a post in the center of the room.

*Jamison said this was a Spanish Mission. This room must be where the Catholic priests kept slaves that rebelled, and the post is where they flogged the worst offenders.*

He opened a large wooden door set in one wall and stepped out into another tunnel.

This one looked like it had seen much use. Metal brackets to hold torches lined both sides of the walls, and as he moved down the hallway, other rooms opened off each side. Up ahead, he saw a glimmer of light. He walked toward it and came to a narrow opening. Thick brush blocked it from the outside, but he pushed through.

In front of him stood a redwood grove with the great trees coming right up to the entrance, hiding the opening.

*I will find brothers who will join me, and we will dance the Ghost Dance here until we are strong enough to drive the whites from the plains.*

Red Bull stepped back into the tunnel and retraced his steps to the last room leading into the hidden passage. He spoke out loud as he stood in the room. "When I have the power of my ancestors, I will have great medicine." Such thoughts filled his mind as he made his way back to the ladder. He would not tell Jamison but would keep this great secret for himself and a trusted few of his brothers.

Las Vegas Jimmy sat in a cold sweat in the back seat of Vinnie's Caddy between Vinnie and a rather large and intimidating thug. The driver headed out of town. Terrible thoughts ran through his brain. *Man, I am dead meat! How am I going to get out of this?*

An old warrior sat on a horse beside the road as Vinnie sped past. The old man smiled. Then, the war bonnet changed into a helmet, the buckskin shirt became a leather jacket, and the old warrior and his horse transformed into a uniformed motorcycle cop on a full-dress Harley Davidson. He turned on the flashing red lights and chased down the thugs.

# CHAPTER SIXTEEN
## SPIRIT DANCERS

Grandma had been reading Red Bull's journal for about a half hour. She set it down and suggested they all have lunch. Grandma and Grandpa whipped up ham sandwiches while the girls poured lemonade.

After lunch, they gathered again in the living room in front of the fireplace. This time Grandpa took up the journal and read where Grandma had left off.

> I kept my secret from Jamison. I had heard of one group, the Bole Maru, who were dancing the spirit dance, and I resolved to find them.

**August 1891**

Red Bull slipped through the shadows behind a small cabin on the outskirts of Sebastopol, a town north of Petaluma, to meet a Pomo named Richard Taylor, leader of the Bole Maru. He'd learned about Taylor from a Pomo who worked on Jamison's ranch, and the man had been the go-between for setting up a meeting. A single light burned in the window—the pre-arranged signal letting Red Bull know Taylor was home. Quickly circling the house to make sure no one was watching, he slipped up to the back door and knocked twice.

The door opened, and a quiet voice said, "Come in, my brother, quickly."

Red Bull stepped inside. Taylor, an older, white-haired man, pointed to a chair at a rickety table, and the two men sat down.

"I am Richard Taylor," he said. "And I understand you are a Ghost Dancer."

Red Bull nodded. "I learned the dance from Wovoka himself when I journeyed to Nevada."

Taylor smiled. "We learned the dance from Wovoka's father ten years before it came to the Sioux. We too seek to connect with the spirits of our ancestors, help bring about the end of the present slavery of our people, and usher in the earth's restoration."

"Will you dance with me, Taylor?"

Taylor shrugged. "We cannot, for the white man watches our villages and homes. They fear that we will rise like you did at Wounded Knee."

"My family is hiding with a man named Jamison in Petaluma," Red Bull said quietly. "I found a secret room under Jamison's ranch. I think the Spanish priests built them to store food and supplies and keep their slaves. A tunnel leads deep into the hill and to a large room where we could dance undisturbed. What better place than right under the white man's nose?"

Taylor looked at Red Bull for a long moment. "Is yours the path of peace or the path of war?"

Red Bull thought for a moment. He knew the Pomo were a weak and scattered tribe and did not dream of warring against the white man. They would only dance to hasten the end of this age. Red Bull needed dancers to dance with him if he were to gain the medicine of the ancestors, so he chose his words with care.

"I wish what you wish, Taylor. I wish the end of inequality, where the true people are no longer cast down but take their rightful place in this land."

Taylor nodded. "Then I and my brothers will dance with you."

Red Bull smiled. Soon he would have big medicine, and then he would lead his people against the whites.

One week later, on a dark, moonless night, Red Bull led a group of Pomos to the tunnel in the Redwood grove. They made their way to the secret room at the bottom of the stairs. Torches in holders on the wall lit the room. A bitter-smelling smoke filled the air.

The group of silent figures joined hands to create a circle. A dead tree branch decorated with religious offerings stood in the center of the formation.

One man sat down and beat the drum, the tempo slow and rhythmic. The dancers did a shuffling counterclockwise side-step, chanting while they danced. The tempo increased.

Round and round the dancers went. Hours passed. Then one figure fell to the ground, rolling around and moaning. The rest of the dancers continued dancing, mesmerized by the beat of the drum. They danced without rest, on and on. From time to time, another dancer, exhausted and dizzy, fell unconscious into the center and lay there as if dead.

After a while, many lay about unconscious. The dancing continued far into the night. Red Bull wore the great medicine shirt. He danced and danced, but he did not receive the vision.

At last, frustrated, he cried out, "I want to see the ancestors. Come now!" At that moment, Red Bull felt a dark presence come into the room. A greenish mist filled the air. The dancers who were still awake cried out in fear. Taylor and his men ran for the stairs, but the presence focused on Red Bull.

Red Bull backed against the wall as eerie figures formed in the mist and closed in around him. "Who are you and what do you want?" he cried out.

"Do not fear," a heart-chilling, menacing voice spoke from out of the mist. "We are your ancestors, and we come to help you kill the white man."

Red Bull wanted to believe, but something in his heart told him these beings were evil and not good.

"Come, Red Bull, let us enter your body, and we will give you great power."

Red Bull grabbed a torch from a holder and inched along the wall, trying to keep the spirits at bay and get to the door. His foot slipped, and he slid down a steep hole at the base of the wall he hadn't seen before. He tumbled into a small room below the dancing room.

"Don't go in there," shrieked the voice from above him. "We cannot follow you."

He could hear the spirits howling with rage above him and shrieking, "What have you to do with us, Son of Man. Go away and leave us in peace."

Red Bull stood and held up the torch. He saw a niche cut into one wall of the room, and in the niche was a silver cross. A silver cup and two candlesticks stood at the base of the cross. The air in the room was different—cleaner and brighter. He stumbled to the foot of the cross. Whatever power was holding the demons at bay was here, around the cross.

He reached out toward the cross and fell unconscious on the floor.

The motorcycle cop looked in the window at Vinnie's driver. "Going to a fire, buddy?"

"Just gimme the ticket and get on with it, okay?" The thug scowled.

"Oh, a wise guy, huh? All right, everybody out of the car." The cop stepped back.

"Wait, what did we do? You got nothin' on us," Vinnie protested.

"Put your hands in plain sight and step out of the car," the cop said, his voice now holding a new and dangerous tone.

Vinnie nodded to his men. "Okay, okay. Don't get all bent out of shape."

The four men got out of the car. Las Vegas Jimmy had a burst of hope in his gut, but Vinnie had a steel grip on his arm.

The cop had his hand close to his revolver. "Turn around and put your hands up on the hood."

The four men turned and leaned on the car.

The next thing Jimmy remembered was a sound like a two-by-four hitting a watermelon. All three of the gangsters went down. He stared at them in amazement.

"Jimmy, turn around." The voice of the cop now sounded different as he spoke.

Slowly, Jimmy turned around.

The cop was changing and glowed with a strange radiance.

Jimmy rubbed his eyes. For a moment, the cop looked like an old Native American, but now he was growing until he became a tall, powerful man about fifteen feet tall with a flaming sword in his hand. Brilliant light shone all around him.

The radiant being spoke. "Someone has sent me to give you an offer you shouldn't refuse. Someone who loves you is asking you to give up your evil ways and live a different life."

"Who is this guy?" Jimmy cried out. "Show me where he is."

The flaming sword swept around in an arc until it pointed down the road toward Petaluma. "Go to the home of James and Rose Roberts and ask them. They will show you the one who desires to help you."

With a booming clap of thunder and a blinding flash of light, the being disappeared.

Jimmy rubbed his eyes and then looked down at the three thugs lying unconscious on the ground. The hair rose on the back of his neck, and he backed away. He turned and ran down the road toward Ghost Dancer Ranch.

# CHAPTER SEVENTEEN
## THE WAY OF PEACE

Everybody took a deep breath when Grandpa finished reading the part about Red Bull's encounter with the evil spirits.

Punkin, Boo, and Jack looked at each other in amazement, for they had met the same evil ones down in the Ghost Dance room.

Grandpa turned the page and read the final entry in the journal.

> When I awoke, I was in my bed in the attic of John Jamison's house. When I opened my eyes, I saw my wife, Chumani, and my daughter, Hantaywee seated beside my bed, and they looked worried.

**August 1891**

Red Bull looked around and saw Jamison standing at the foot of the bed. His wife and daughter were there too. "How did I get here?"

Jamison pointed to the door to the secret passage. "I was in the shaft, working on the ladder, and I heard the drums coming up the passage. I knew you were down in the tunnels doing the Ghost Dance."

Red Bull closed his eyes. "You knew about the tunnels?"

"Sure." Jamison laughed. "After Mariano sold me this place, I had a visit from a priest who used to serve in the old mission when he was young. He took me to the tunnel behind the Redwood grove and showed me all the passages. Those rooms with the chains were where they kept Pomos they used for slave labor to build the mission. A lot of bad stuff happened down there, and the old priest made a full confession. I guess he wanted to get it off his chest. When I heard the screams down there tonight, I came running. Sounded like you were in a heap of trouble."

"How did I get here?"

"Well, you were pretty incoherent, but you were able to move. So, I got you up here." Jamison smiled. "It was tough. You're a big man."

"What were those things we conjured up?"

Jamison shrugged. "Well, I reckon those were evil spirits that used to make that place a home when all the bad stuff was happening."

"The messiah, Wovoka, told us that if we called upon the spirits of our ancestors, they would bring in the new earth, a place of peace. But those spirits were evil. I don't understand."

"Well, Red Bull, I guess you had to see for yourself. The Bible tells me the Creator God thinks it's a bad thing to call up the spirits of the dead, and for just the reason you described. There are many evil spirits waiting to take advantage of humans. They love to take over human bodies so they can walk the earth and damage God's creation. I think you ran into a few of those guys masquerading as your ancestors."

Red Bull remembered the horrible feeling when they had surrounded him. "They were bad *Manitou,* snake spirits. They wanted to come into me, to possess me. What stopped them?"

"When I found you, you were down in the little room under the dancing room. I think my God protected you by showing you how to get there. You were lying there, reaching out to the cross and passed out cold. Took a bit to wake you up."

"What power is in the cross to drive off evil spirits?" Red Bull asked.

"Well, my friend, it isn't so much what's in the cross, but who it represents. There is a Messiah. But it isn't old Wovoka. The real Messiah's name is Jesus, and he came over eighteen hundred years ago to save every man, woman, boy, and girl on this planet from the things that kept them from knowing him. We call those things sin, and the most common sin is when we think we can live our lives without God's help, but it's all the bad things that people do to each other too. Like the way us white folks have treated other folks, and the way they've treated us back. Jesus saved us all by dying in our place on the cross."

"Is that why you are so kind to my family, Jamison?"

"Yes, Red Bull. I've given my life and heart to the true Messiah, and the Bible tells me that if I love him, I will keep his commands. I do love him and try to do what he says, but sometimes it's awful hard. The good news is that he sent his Spirit—a good Spirit called the Holy Spirit—to live in me and to help me walk in kindness and love. It's not even so much that Jesus tells me to love people who are hurt, he tells me to love everyone. So, when I saw that you needed help, it was my duty as a Christian to take you in."

Hantaywee looked at Jamison. "Does this Jesus love me too?"

Jamison smiled. "Well, the Bible says God so loved everyone in the world he gave Jesus to us as a gift, and that anybody who believed in Jesus would never die but have everlasting life."

Red Bull suddenly realized the truth. "Then what Wovoka told us was just a lie made up by a man trying to take Jesus's place. Jamison, if this God you serve teaches you to love like you have loved me and my family, I want to know him too."

"Well, Chief, that's just as easy as asking him to be with you forever and to forgive all the bad things you've ever done. Do you want to do that?"

Red Bull nodded. "Yes."

"I too wish to know this Jesus," Chumani said.

"And I," Hantaywee said.

There in the room the three of them knelt beside the bed and held hands with Red Bull as they began the greatest journey they would ever take.

Grandpa put down the journal and reached for a hanky in his back pocket.

Grandma sat with tears running down her face.

"I have been searching for the answer for many years," Jack Wilson said in a shaky voice. "And here in Red Bull's journal, I find the way of peace for my people. Do you think Jesus would forgive me too?"

Punkin and Boo looked at each other and grinned.

Grandma put her arm around Jack's shoulder. "It's no mistake you came here, Jack. Like Grandpa Jamison told Red Bull, it's just as easy as asking."

A knock sounded on the door.

Grandma looked up. "Who could that be?" He got up and went to the door.

A man stood there, looking tired and forlorn. He looked at Grandpa with an awkward smile on his face. "I'm Jimmy, the guy trying to steal your ranch. This sounds crazy, but I think I met an angel, and he sent me here to find out about some guy who can help me change my ways. I'm sorry that I did you folks wrong, and I want to make amends."

Grandpa took Jimmy by the arm and led him inside. "Well, Jimmy, there was a day when I would have been a mite upset about you trying to kill me."

"I know, Mr. Roberts, and I'm sorry for that. I want to make up for it. Can you help me?"

"It's a funny thing, Jimmy, because your timing couldn't be better. We're having a revival meeting right now. Why don't you join us?"

Later that day, Jack Wilson was talking with Grandma and Grandpa. "I was hoping to find the Ghost Dancer shirt, Mr. Roberts, but I found much more. I still wonder if it's here, though."

Grandpa grinned. "You know, Jack, there was a little more that I didn't read from Red Bull's journal. He gave directions for finding the shirt. He said he left his old life at the foot of the cross, and he put down Matthew 13:44, which is the parable of the treasure hidden in the field. There was also a note in there about how Hantaywee and John fell in love and married soon after."

"Hantaywee changed her name to Ruth," Grandma added. "And at their wedding, she said these words for her vow: 'Entreat me not to leave thee, John, or to return from following thee: for whither thou goest, I will go; and where thou lodgest, I will lodge: thy people shall be my people, and thy God my God.' And that was how Red Bull's family and mine joined."

Punkin and Boo had come into the room while Grandpa and Jack were talking. Boo pulled on Grandpa's arm. "Can we all go look for the shirt?"

"Sure, honey," he answered. "I don't think there's any danger now."

Punkin gave Boo a little push. "Yeah, Boo, just remember that Scripture you quoted about 'greater is he' and we'll be okay."

Gathering up flashlights and shovels, Jack led everyone back to the "dance hall" as Grandpa called it. The room seemed much lighter than the last time Jack had been there. No sense of the evil presence that had once lived there lingered. They squeezed through the narrow passage into the lower room.

Jack walked over to the cross. "Red Bull said he left his old life at the foot of the cross, so we should dig here." He and Grandpa dug below the silver cross.

In a few minutes, they heard a thump as Jack's shovel struck something. They all gathered as Jack cleaned the dirt off an old metal chest. He got it out of the ground and set it in the middle of the room.

Grandpa opened the lid.

A bundle wrapped in oilcloth lay on top of something else. Grandpa pulled out the bundle and handed it to Grandma.

Grandma handed it to Jack. "Would you do the honors, please?"

Jack unrolled the bundle and held up the shirt of old Red Bull.

Punkin pointed to a spot on the front of the shirt. "Look at the place over the heart!"

Where the eagle had once flown, someone had cut it out and patched in another piece—a simple cross.

Boo spoke up. "The piece of cloth attached to the key to the carved box. Red Bull cut it out and replaced it with a cross to show he found the true way."

Jack pointed into the box. "Look at this." In the bottom of the box, a silver cup lay on top of a heap of golden coins. A letter accompanied it. Boo opened it and read.

This is the Ghost Dancer shirt. Red Bull and I decided it would be dangerous if it fell into the wrong hands. So, we hid it here. And as for the gold, I believe the Lord told me that somewhere down the line a member of my family would need it. So, I've left it as a gift. May it be a blessing to a member of my family.

John Jamison

Grandma stared at the gold. "James, this should pay all of our bills and give us enough in the bank so we never need to sell the ranch. I feel like singing."

Grandpa nodded. "Lead us, Rose."

"Praise God from whom all blessings flow," she began.

Grandpa, Boo, and Punkin joined in. "Praise Him all creatures here below. Praise Him above ye heavenly host. Praise Father, Son and Holy Ghost. Amen."

The words of the old hymn of praise filled the ancient Ghost Dance room. Punkin and Boo would have been surprised to see how many angels filled the room above them, listening in wonder as the five people joined their hearts and gave honest and simple thanks to God.

And they would have been more surprised to see an old Native American man leading all the angels in praise to the God who reigned over Ghost Dancer Ranch.

# CHAPTER EIGHTEEN
## AFTERWARD

Springtime once again came to Petaluma. Almost seven months had passed since the girl's summer vacation turned into an exciting adventure. Tall green grass, and yellow acacia blossoms were bursting out on the hillsides, and the Scotch broom was budding up the canyons.

John Roberts drove the family station wagon through the gate at the old Ghost Dancer Ranch and pulled up to the house as Grandma and Grandpa Roberts walked out onto the big rambling porch.

Punkin ran down the steps behind them and pulled open the back door of the car.

Boo jumped out, and the two girls hugged each other. "Punkin! it is so good to see you again!"

"Yes, Boo, it's good to see you too."

The two girls hugged again.

Boo looked up at the old house and put her arm around Punkin's shoulders. "It seems like forever since we solved the mystery of the ranch. So much has happened since then—exciting stuff."

"What, Boo?"

"Well, Punkin, I asked Grandma not to tell you so I could surprise you. When my Dad got the job in Texas, the first thing that happened was that his company got sold to a bigger company. One condition of Dad keeping his job was that he transfers to California. Santa Rosa, to be exact."

Punkin jumped up and down. "What? You're moving to Santa Rosa? That's only twenty miles from Petaluma."

"Yeah, but you live in Marin. That's a long way." Boo frowned.

"I have news for you too, Boo. My Dad got hired as the pastor of a new church in Petaluma, and we're moving here."

"Wow. That's means we can see a lot of each other."

Carol got out of the car and came up beside the cousins. "How about if we start this summer? We're planning a vacation up the coast to Mendocino to an area called 'The Lost Coast,' and John has to research property there for his company. We'll rent a beach house and asked your family to come along."

"Yay!" the girls shouted together.

Just then, a young man stepped out onto the porch.

"Jack Wilson! How are you?" Boo ran up the steps to greet him

Pops grinned. "You can call him Pastor Jack now."

"I'm not a pastor yet." He turned a little red. "But I'm being discipled and studying the Bible and taking classes online."

"We've given Jack's tribe a piece of the ranch to build a church," Grams chimed in. "on the condition he studies to be the pastor and uses his leadership gifts to help his people."

Jack pointed to a small building on the other side of the lake. "We're building it now. I've really seen Jesus is the best way I can help my people. I still deeply love and appreciate my own customs and history, but I know now that Jesus came for everyone and that all of us—the white man and Native American, yellow and black—are sinners who need a Savior. And I will help my people discover the truth."

At that moment, three men came around the barn.

"Where do you want the lumber stacked, Pastor?" the oldest man asked.

Boo stared in astonishment. "Running Horse, Weasel!"

"Please, Boo," Joe said, ducking his head as if embarrassed, "those are names we left behind. We are Peter and John now, and we're doing our best to make up for all we've done wrong."

Running Horse nodded. "Yeah. Pastor Jack came and visited us in jail and gave us the good news about Jesus, and we believed him. And when we said yes, the Lord healed both of us. You can see our hair isn't white anymore." He grinned.

Boo looked closer at the third man and couldn't believe her eyes. "Jimmy, is that you?"

"Yes, it's me," Las Vegas Jimmy said, grinning from ear to ear. "After the police arrested me, your Grandpa came and stood up for me in court. They released me into his custody. I'm in a halfway house, but I work here every day. I never knew I had so many muscles that could get sore."

They all laughed.

Grandma herded everyone up the steps. "Let's all go get a glass of lemonade." They went into the house, but Punkin and Boo stayed behind.

Boo took Punkin by the arm. "The Lost Coast. Boy, Punkin, doesn't that sound mysterious?"

"Now, Boo, don't go getting us into another adventure before we even go."

"Oh pancakes, Punkin. Don't be an old scaredy-cat."

"I'm not a scaredy-cat. I'm just as ready for another adventure as you are."

"Well, that's the Punkin I know and love. And I see you're not wearing those fancy outfits anymore."

"Oh you," Punkin cried, and she tried to punch Boo on the shoulder as the two girls ran laughing into the house.

Out by the barn, a dark figure stood smiling.

"The Lost Coast ... sounds interesting. What have you got for us up there, Lord? Okay, I'll wait and see," and the old man disappeared around the corner of the barn. "I'll just wait and see."

# ABOUT THE AUTHOR

**Patrick E. Craig** is the author of seven books. In 2013, Harvest House Publishers published his *Apple Creek Dreams* series. After the series went out of print, Patrick republished it through his own imprint, P&J Publishing, in 2018. His current series is *The Paradise Chronicles* and the first book, *The Amish Heiress* was published in 2015. It remained on the Amazon Top 100 best sellers list for seven months. *The Amish Princess* was released in 2016 followed by *The Mennonite Queen* in 2019. In 2017 Harlequin purchased the print rights for *The Amish Heiress* for their Walmart Amish series. The Harlequin print version went into Walmart stores in April 2019. In March 2019, Patrick signed with Elk Lake Publishers to publish *The Adventures of Punkin and Boo* series. Patrick and his wife, Judy, make their home in Idaho. Patrick is represented by the Steve Laube Agency.

Patrick's website can be found at https://www.patrickecraig.com
facebook.com/PatrickECraig
twitter.com/PatrickECraig

# THE MYSTERY OF GHOST DANCER RANCH

More exciting stories from *The Adventures of Punkin and Boo*.
*The Lost Coast*

A family trip turns into a deadly adventure when Punkin and Boo stumble onto the operations of a ruthless gang of marijuana smugglers on the wild Lost Coast of northern California. When the gang discovers Boo's dad is in town to buy land for a resort, they kidnap the girls' families to keep them from discovering the gang's secret illegal pot gardens. With the help of an undercover DEA agent, the girls escape into the untamed Sinkyone Wilderness.

Pursued by a desperate gangster known only as "El Fuente" and some evil fallen angels, the girls discover anew the reality of God's protecting hand over them and the wonder of lost souls coming to know their Savior. They also find unlooked-for help from some mysterious treasure hunters and their old friend Jack Wilson, as they solve the mystery of the Lost Coast.

They face great danger as they seek to elude the gang, find their parents, and bring the criminals to justice.